STILLWATER LAKE

J.P. CHOQUETTE

J.P. CHOQUETTE

Stillwater Lake

First published by Scared E Cat Books 2022

Copyright © 2022 by J.P. Choquette

First edition

ISBN: 978-1-950976-18-8

This book was professionally typeset on Reedsy.
Find out more at reedsy.com

Chapter 1

Jessica Brown
Stillwater, Vermont

The rattle of the windowpane woke Jessica from an uneasy sleep. The pane shimmied in its wooden frame. She watched it from the slightly sagging mattress. The wind outside whipped at the window and screamed around the eaves. Her heart thundered in her chest. She put a hand there, felt it pound. But why? Had she had a nightmare? She didn't think she'd slept deeply enough for the—she glanced at the alarm clock blearily—past three hours. The green numbers announced it was just after three. She'd tumbled into bed after a third glass of wine and a half-smoked cigarette a little after midnight. She didn't smoke anymore, not for three months. Not usually.

The wind screamed again, like a dying woman. Jessica pushed back the blankets and toed around the floor by the bed for her slippers. They weren't there. She must not have unpacked them yet. Either that, or she'd forgotten them back home.

She shivered and pulled on a ratty sweater. Her "grandpa sweater," Bryan called it. She smiled but it quickly fell away.

Bryan.

1

If only he were here. If only—

"No. Stop it," she said out loud, her voice little more than a mumble. Still, it grounded her. Made her remember. Her head pounded and she put her hand there and massaged her temples lightly. Bryan was gone. He wasn't coming back. Time to get used to it.

Shuffling to the window, Jessica wrapped the sweater around her tightly. Leaning on the rounded log wall close to the window, Jessica peered out. She'd expected blackness—up here in the mountains in the middle of a storm—but a soft bluish glow came from the little grove of pine trees closest to the cabin's front door. Strange. What was making that light? she wondered. An optical illusion, some bit of light from the cabin reflecting onto the trees, maybe.

Sitting on the front steps after hauling in her stuff earlier that evening, she'd studied the small knot of trees while enjoying her first glass of wine. They'd felt friendly somehow, safe. Not like the rest of the forest surrounding the cabin. The woods here were wild and untamed. Jessica had been camping twice in her life—once in high school and a second time in college—but she'd never been in a forest like this. It seemed to reach out from all around the cabin toward her: thick, clinging vines threatened to choke her while huge trees with jagged boughs pointed their accusing fingers at her. Even the low-lying brush underfoot was thick and impenetrable. Jessica shivered at the thought of hiking in the wooded area.

The faint glow of light had dimmed. Jessica pressed her face closer to the glass. The windowpane shivered and Jessica took an involuntary step back.

"Chicken." She could almost hear Bryan's teasing voice. She ran a hand over her face and sagged back against the wall.

Bang!

Something hit the window hard.

Jessica screamed. She looked wildly toward the pane of glass but saw only a smudge in the next lightning flash. Hand still over her mouth, she looked again toward the blueish light but it was completely gone. The night was shades of gray and black and all around her, the trees swayed toward the cabin and then away.

She stepped away from the window, feeling suddenly exposed. What had hit it? A bat maybe. Or a branch. Birds didn't fly at night, did they? Unless it was an owl. Nighthawks. Did they have those here in Vermont? Jessica rubbed her hands over her arms, fingers catching intermittently on the misshapen fibers of the sweater. Her hands trembled like a newborn bird.

"You're being a complete baby," she told herself.

Still, there was no point in going back to bed. She'd never fall back to sleep. She might as well make tea and do some more unpacking. *Yes, like your laptop,* a little voice—not Bryan's this time—chimed in. *Why hasn't that been unpacked yet?* She ignored it and retreated from the window.

The upper floor of the small log cabin was a half loft, a feature that Jessica had loved when seeing it on the house rental website. She walked down the stairs, held tightly to the cold railing. The winding wrought iron staircase emptied into the living room. The entire bottom floor of the cabin was an open space. The living room opened into a small eat-in kitchen. A tiny half bath sat on the other side. There was a single entrance to the cabin—the front door was in the kitchen. She'd wondered when she'd seen if it was a fire hazard but hadn't bothered to ask before booking.

Jessica put a robin's egg blue teakettle on the back burner.

3

She turned on the gas, held her breath until the flame caught. While she waited for the teakettle to boil, she sat at the table and surveyed the boxes and bags yet to be unpacked.

"It's perfect," Theresa had gushed when Jessica had told her agent of her plan. "Just what you need. If you can't get your mojo back there, I don't know what to tell you!"

But Jessica didn't need Theresa to tell her. If her writing muse didn't show up at the cabin, deep in the wilderness. Jessica knew the outcome. She'd lose more fans. Her business accounts would hemorrhage more money, faster than they had already been. She'd run the risk of being what every best-selling author feared: a has-been.

"That's not going to happen," Theresa had said when Jessica had voiced this. "You're too good of an author, too much of a professional to let it. You're not some two-bit, pulp fiction writer. You're Claudia Snow! You are the face of romance writing today. Who was it who won the RITA just two years ago? The Romance Writers of America don't hand those trophies out willy-nilly, sweets."

Jessica had taken an extra-large swallow of wine. "I should tape you saying this and play it back when I get blocked," she'd said, only half-joking.

"And which author has graced the *New York Times* bestseller list for twenty-six weeks in the last twelve months?" Theresa had reminded her without pause.

"But that was before," Jessica had said. She didn't have to finish the sentence. Theresa knew what she was talking about. Before Bryan—

"Here's where I tell you the difference between fact and fiction, Jessica," Theresa's voice had the same hard, no-nonsense tone that had terrified Jessica as a younger writer. "You're brilliant as a writer. But more importantly, you are relatable. Fans love you—the real you—even if they only know you through your pen name. You are a gifted storyteller. Period. And you're meant for this career, for this, this..." there had been a pause as Theresa had tried to find the right words, "Life. You were meant to be a novelist, and you are one. A damned good one. And one personal upset—however much it hurts—is not going to take that away," Theresa's voice had softened then. "Not unless you let it, sweets."

Jessica had sighed. Theresa was right. Most of the time her agent was. Jessica had learned that too as a younger author and she'd told Theresa then.

"Of course, I am," Theresa had said. "That's what makes me such a stellar agent. And what makes you so lucky to have me," she'd laughed, that deep, resonating chuckle that belied her pack-a-day habit for the past thirty years.

"Take your time. Well," Theresa had made a face. "Not too much. Remember, the draft is due in September. But now..." She'd lit a cigarette. "Now you have to tackle your to-do list. I'm sure that you have a lot of details to take care of before you leave."

And Jessica had. She'd funneled her fear and sadness into packing boxes and bags and suitcases. She'd taken care of the million and one things that needed to be taken care of before going on a three-month hiatus: stopping the mail, notifying her twice-a-week housekeeper, and calling the head of the local school where Jessica volunteered as a writing coach once a week. So many complicated details required to free herself up for an uncomplicated visit to the country! No wonder she couldn't write. There were too many balls in the air, too many obligations tying her down.

That's what she'd told herself anyway. That there, in the wilderness, she'd find the solace and peace she was craving. That she'd clear her mind enough to refresh her creativity. She needed it desperately to start the next book.

The teakettle screeched. Jessica lurched to her feet, snatched it from the burner, and turned off the flame. Her heartbeat, which had slowed slightly, hammered again in her chest. She steadied herself on the counter and then dug through the nearest box, looking for teabags.

Five minutes later, she sat on the cream-colored couch in the living room. Outside the wind continued to whip and now rain pelted hard against the cabin. She watched the storm with her eyes, but her mind was still on the cracked windowpane upstairs. What could have hit the glass hard enough to do that? And what had caused the light coming from the little grove of pine trees? She adjusted her position, feeling vulnerable with the curtains open but fascinated too by the power of the storm.

"I'd put something in front of that door at night," Lydia, the teen who'd helped her unpack the SUV had told Jessica earlier that afternoon. Jessica, exhausted after the seven-hour drive, had only been half-listening as Lydia had droned on about things to do in the area. She'd sounded like a mechanical puppet, repeating the words that Jessica was sure Lydia's mother, the owner of the rental agency, required her to give each guest.

"Why would I do that?" Jessica had stopped struggling with the last box and slid it across the floor toward the kitchen with her high-heeled sandal. "The door has a lock doesn't it?"

"Yeah, it's got a lock," Lydia had said, licking her lips. "But," she'd stopped then, glancing over her shoulder theatrically, as though looking for someone offstage. "That wouldn't stop the gargun."

"The gargun?"

"Sure. You've never heard of him?"

Jessica had sighed then, blowing air out of her nose and sinking onto the biggest box close by. "No, I can't say as I have."

"I thought that's why you came here. For the gargun festival."

"He really must be famous if you have a whole festival for him," Jessica had said.

Lydia had smiled politely. Jessica was ready for Lydia to go. She wanted nothing more than to fill up the tub with the hottest water she could stand and a glass of ice-cold water and lemon and wash the trip off of her. But she also remembered what it was like to be Lydia's age. To feel like no one really saw you or listened to you.

Jessica took a big breath and asked, "So, what's a gargun?"

"There are a few different theories about him," Lydia had admitted. "But the one most people agree with is that it's a sea monster. But not huge—like the Loch Ness Monster. Or Champ—that's the monster in Lake Champlain. He's more like a cross between a monster and a man. Like, he can come out of the water and walk around and stuff."

"Oh. Well, that's handy," Jessica stood and dusted off her hands. Hopefully, Lydia would get the hint. "And the festival is a parade or something?"

"Nope," Lydia had shaken her head. "The Gargun Festival draws people from all over the country, some even from further than that," she'd grinned. "We get the bulk of our summer traffic from it. It's the biggest tourist attraction that Stillwater offers."

Jessica had held in a groan. She'd come here to get away from the crowds, away from people. To concentrate on her book, not get roped into some country bumpkin festival.

"I doubt I'll be affected much, being way out here," Jessica had said.

But Lydia had shaken her head, disagreeing. "Not with the festival traffic, no. But the gargun?" She shrugged. "He likes it best by the water—it's where he lives. But some people say that he likes the woods too. Remote places. Far from watchful eyes. He stalks his prey quietly, so quietly you'd never even know he was there. And then—"

A two-way radio on the girl's hip had squawked as though on cue.

"Doogle?" a woman's voice asked.

Jessica had jumped, startled and Lydia had snatched up the radio, pushing the button before she even brought it to her lips.

"Mom, please," she'd said, irritation in her voice.

"Sorry, I forgot. Lydia. Are you almost finished? The Wrights are arriving soon, and I need you to open the place up, and air it out. I hope you explained how much I wanted to be there for Ms. Brown's arrival."

Lydia glanced at Jessica who smiled back.

"Tell her everything is wonderful," Jessica had said. "I appreciate your help. But I'm all set now, really. Just going to relax after the long trip."

Lydia had stared at her a moment longer than necessary, then fingered the button on the radio.

"Ms. Brown thinks everything's wonderful, Mom. And yes, I'm on my way," she'd said into the gray box. "Be there in ten." Lydia's long dirty-blonde hair was tied into a messy bun and it had wobbled on her head as she'd re-fastened the shortwave to her shorts.

"Well, I'd better go. The cabin the Wrights are renting is huge so it'll take forever to air it out before I check them in."

8

"Do you have many guests?"

Lydia had shrugged. "Now we do. The festival is the biggest draw all year. But we don't have as many guests as my mom would like. The Wrights are from somewhere out west—Chicago, I think—they have a couple of kids." She made a face. "Families with kids are the worst. Cleaning the place out after a family's been there sucks, especially if the kids are little. There's always Cheerios mushed everywhere and no one ever remembers to empty the garbage before they go which reek of dirty diapers. I mean, seriously? How hard is it to drop the garbage off at the dumpster when you check out?"

She'd paused, looked around the space again as though really seeing it for the first time. For a moment Jessica thought Lydia was going to grill her on her housekeeping abilities.

Instead, Lydia glanced toward the driveway.

"Anyway, if you need anything, you can get in touch with Mom. She explained about the cell signal?"

Jessica had nodded.

"Right. About ten minutes by car, twenty-five or so on foot. You'll come to the crest just before the mountain starts to descend. There's a good spot there for a pretty clear signal. I could always ask Mom about getting you a radio—"

"No, thank you, that won't be necessary. It's one of the reasons I came out here, to get away from instant communication. And thanks for your help this afternoon." Jessica had flipped open her Gucci wallet and extracted two twenties, pressing them into the younger woman's hand. "I appreciate it."

Lydia's eyes widened. "Hey, no problem. Thank you!"

She'd jogged from the small porch to a battered Land Rover and climbed in. With a hurried wave, she'd backed out of the small parking area near a flower bed, spewing gravel in her wake after she gave it a little too much gas.

Jessica had closed the door and started the bath water. A long, hot soak would get rid of that travel feeling.

It wasn't until now that Jessica had thought about what Lydia had said.

About the gargun.

And putting something heavy in front of the cabin's door.

Jessica swallowed and glanced toward the window. Outside, the trees continued their menacing dance. But there was another sound besides the wind moaning around the cabin. Something like a heavy tread over the stones in the driveway. Was she imagining it? She closed her eyes, tried to hear more clearly, but the wind made that impossible.

If she was brave like the heroines in her books, she'd storm outdoors with a broom or an ax or some other makeshift weapon and demand to know who was out there. Instead, heart thumping, Jessica dragged the small kitchen table to the front door. Then she shoved its solid bulk against it, feeling better.

Chapter 2

Lydia Donovan

Lydia grunted as she stood up and stretched her back. She'd been weeding the flower bed in front of the office for over an hour. It felt more like twelve. She glanced around, seeing if anyone from school was in the vicinity. But Main Street was quiet, like usual. Lines of paint-faded shops, a bakery, two churches, two gas stations, and a rundown brick building that housed City Hall looked the same as always.

Hearing squeals from kids at the town pool a street over she wished very hard that she was there. Alex Richards was a lifeguard there this summer. Lydia knew because her best friend's cousin had mentioned it at a dance two months ago. Since then, Lydia had been trying to think of ways to get to the pool more often. Swim lessons maybe? But of course, there wasn't money for that. And her mother had other plans for Lydia's summer.

"If you're going to work for me, you're going to work." Her mother's voice had been low but urgent-sounding. Lydia had been offended at first. She knew she was a hard worker. Many of her mother's friends had said the same over the years.

Her mother had sighed like she often did these days.

"The truth is, Doogle, we're in a bit of a bad place financially. I've been doing the best I can but without the staff…" Her voice had drifted away. Lydia had known what her mother meant then.

Ever since Dad had left, there hadn't been enough of anything: not enough money, not enough help, not enough time. And though Lydia would never tell her mother this, she secretly wondered if her mother had the business sense that had come so naturally to her father. Unfortunately, Dad had been great at selling things other than rental properties to out-of-staters. He'd eventually charmed the business's one full-time employee—the office manager/housekeeper—right into his arms. He and Samantha had left town, headed to Vegas. And left Mom and Lydia to pick up the pieces.

She felt the familiar sharp fingernail of pain in her chest that she felt whenever she thought of Dad. Such a jerk! Leaving them in the lurch with a business that, while hadn't been booming, had at least been doing better financially. Over the past two years, things had gotten gloomier. That's why it was so important that they fill every rental they could this summer. It wasn't a problem over Gargun Festival weekend. Then, all the hotels, cabins, and even campgrounds were packed. But the festival only lasted a week. What about the rest of summer?

"Almost done, Doogle?" Lydia's mother appeared at the screen door of the office. Lydia didn't bother to correct her.

"It looks great," she said, not waiting for Lydia's reply. "I'm sorry I've been so distracted today. The people that rented Cedar had a death in the family and had to cancel. I've been trying to see if I can switch around another reservation to get it rented out. It means offering a discount but," her mother shrugged.

Cedar was their priciest property, a full-sized house complete with a wrap-around porch and gorgeous views of the lake. It was usually also the most popular rental. It had a lot of bedrooms and even a clubhouse for the kids. There was a small pond in the backyard stocked with fish.

"Bummer," Lydia said. "Mom, can I finish this tomorrow? My back is killing me."

Her mother smiled at her. She looked tired, Lydia thought, like she had every day since Dad had left.

"Sure, Doog—uh, honey. Thanks for all your hard work today. I was on the phone when you got back from the Wrights'. Everything all right there?"

Lydia nodded. "Yeah. They're total royals but everything else was fine."

"You know I don't like that, Lydia. These people pay our mortgage. Someday you're going to slip up and say it in front of one of them and then you'll have to explain what a 'royal' is."

Lydia tried to look abashed but doubted she was successful. Her and Katie had come up with the term. Being local meant the girls often felt like the servants working below stairs. Royals were the worst of the city people—the ones who treated you like an annoying insect.

All Lydia wanted now was to call Katie and get to the pool. Maybe it was Alex's afternoon to work. Maybe he was right now slathering himself with suntan oil and looking casually around the pool, checking to see if Lydia was there. She got a weird feeling in her stomach at the thought.

"Sorry," she said now to her mother.

Her mother tried to maintain her frown, but Lydia could see it was a struggle. "All right. Well, you're free until dinner. We're having leftover hotdogs."

"Again?"

"The package that the last family left in Cedar was huge. I froze some. So, yes. Again." Her mother looked out at Main Street. Then she asked without turning her head, "What are you going to do after your shower?"

Lydia shrugged. "I'll call Katie now, see what she's doing. Maybe we'll head over to the pool." She tried to keep her voice nonchalant but her mother with her super-Mom powers immediately picked up on it.

"I heard Victoria Richards say that her son's working there this summer. What's his name again? Andrew? Arthur?"

Lydia laughed. "Arthur? Mom, no one names their kid that anymore."

"Well, what is it, smarty pants?"

"Alex."

"Oh, that's right. Alex." Her mother wiggled her eyebrows up and down. Lydia pretended not to notice. Her traitor cheeks turned hot though, and her stomach felt even weirder.

"We don't really have money for the pool—"

"I got a tip this morning. From Ms. Brown." Lydia interrupted and then wished she hadn't said anything. She couldn't remember the last time she'd had forty bucks all to herself. She knew what Mom was going to say. "You know that any money that comes into your hands comes into the business. I can't float this boat on my own." But there were so many things Lydia wanted to buy! New earbuds because hers were making a crackling sound every time she tried to listen to her antique iPod, nail polish, a fresh copy of *Vogue* magazine—

"Oh, I forgot to ask how that went. She's all settled in?"

Lydia nodded. Maybe if she talked to Mom about Ms. Brown, her mother would forget about the giant tip crinkled in Lydia's back pocket.

"She's really nice. But she seems kinda private. I offered to help her unpack, but she didn't want me to. And then I offered her one of your shortwave radios—you know, the emergency ones—but she didn't want one of those either."

"You can't offer those out, hon," her mother said. "We need them for real emergencies."

Lydia shrugged. "I know, but she's all alone up there. And with the gargun—"

"You didn't tell her those silly stories, did you?" Her mother's voice had raised two octaves, a sure sign she was getting stressed.

"Oh, uh. Well—"

"Lydia!"

"It just sort of slipped out. I mean, Mom, it's not like she's not going to hear about it. The festival starts this Friday anyway."

"Yes, but that just celebrates the G-rated version of the gargun. Let's not scare our summer visitors or spread around a lot of stupid old wives' tales."

Her mother had always hated hearing about the gargun. Ironic since without it, the summer festival wouldn't happen, and a solid portion of their summer business would dry up. It was Dad who'd loved the old legend: telling Lydia and her friends the stories his father had told him. Going out on the lake alone in the early morning and late evenings, Dad had hoped to catch a glimpse of the gargun himself. At least, that's what he'd told his family. Who knows? Maybe his affair with Samantha had been going on longer than either of them had admitted.

"Sorry," Lydia said again. She dug in her pocket, pulled out the forty dollars. She hesitated for the briefest second before handing it over to her mother.

15

"Here," she said.

Her mother sighed again and looked from Lydia's hand to her face and back again. Finally, she leaned forward and took the money from her daughter's fingers, then put one of the twenties back in Lydia's hand.

"You keep that. You've been working hard and I appreciate it. I know that I don't give you enough—you'd make more working at the general store or babysitting—but I'm glad you're helping me out. You're my right-hand woman, right?"

Lydia smiled and pocketed the cash. "Right."

"Well, I need to get back to the books. Dinner's at six sharp."

Lydia nodded. Dinner was always at six sharp, but she didn't remind her mother that she already knew this. Instead, she headed toward the half of the building that was their family home and climbed the stairs. Her legs were tired, but she was tempted to dance up to the shower anyway. Maybe Lydia could borrow a suit from Katie. Lydia's old, ratty one was totally embarrassing. And maybe Alex would ask her out on a date. Who knew what the afternoon held?

Chapter 3

Tony Bradford

Tony checked the GPS unit again but saw the same thing: a little blue bar that read, "searching" like it had been for the past forty minutes. He stuffed it back into his pants pocket and kept going. He'd known the cell signal was spotty but had hoped the GPS would work better. So far, no luck.

The sunrise over the mountain had been amazing though. He was glad he'd made the trek. But now the sun beat down and sweat dripped in itchy, meandering paths down his neck and back. He wanted nothing more than to get back to his cabin and jump in the shower. Or the lake, whichever was coldest.

Dreaming of an icy cold glass of fresh water laden with ice cubes, Tony tipped his head back and took a swig from the warm water in his canteen. It tasted faintly of plastic, but he swallowed it. Stuffing the canteen back into his pack, he hefted it back onto his shoulders. He wasn't lost...was he?

Looking around him, Tony could clearly see that he was on a trail. The thing was he didn't know *which* trail. Or how much longer it would be until he was back in town. Or if this particular trail even went to town.

Still, no need to worry. Chances were good he'd just taken a wrong turn higher up on the mountain. A trail was a trail and had to lead somewhere. He walked on for another five minutes or so and checked the GPS again. Still nothing.

He was replacing it in his pocket when he saw something—a bright flash of color. Another hiker?

"Hello?" he called out. "Hello, anyone there?"

The color didn't move though. It was a bright reddish-purple shade.

He stepped off the trail and walked in the direction of the color. Getting closer he realized what it was: a flower. Actually, an entire bed of flowers. They sat in a bed bordering a small gravel area that skirted a driveway. Relief washed over Tony. A cabin nearly blended in with the woods, sitting further back in the trees.

Civilization.

He started to climb down behind the cabin but then thought better of it. What if it was a hunting cabin? He didn't want to "accidentally," get himself shot because he'd surprised some backwoodsman. A backwoodsman who liked to plant flower beds? Tony grinned.

He veered back to the left, kept the small house in sight. He hiked through the trees, brambles and undergrowth caught his clothing. The woods here were incredible. He'd forgotten how wild parts of his home state still were. Pucker brush and other painful-looking thorny vines laced the forest. The canopy overhead was thick—so thick that Tony was surprised the sun could beat down on him at all.

When he'd looked upward earlier it had created a disquieting feeling. It was like looking down into a valley but in reverse. Rather than a meandering river bordered by sheer cliffs, here the tall, tall trees pointed toward a swath of blue sky and the white-hot sun beating down between the branches.

Tony had gotten used to the never-ending sounds of the forest: creaks and groans of the branches rubbing against each other in the trees overhead; the conversation of the birds as they squabbled over territory or maybe called juveniles home for lunch; the soft whistle of wind through pine boughs.

But now a sound broke through the relatively quiet air. Birds stopped mid-chirp as they too heard it. Faintly, a voice was singing. The tune was familiar but so off-key Tony couldn't quite place it. A backwoodsman who planted flowers and sang? His grin widened and loped down the rest of the incline, entering the cabin's driveway. The crushed gravel underfoot was loud so he didn't worry about startling whoever was singing.

As he drew closer, he could see the woman—blonde-haired, sitting reclined in an Adirondack chair on the front porch. She was sprawled over it, her head swayed from side to side as she kept rhythm with some unheard beat. Two white buds poked out of her ears and her voice warbled and sank then reached for another high note. Tony grimaced at the sound.

He drew close to the porch and waved his hands.

"Hello?"

No response.

"Excuse me," he said more loudly and waved his arms vigorously.

The woman, maybe sensing the motion or seeing shadows behind her lids opened her eyes. They went wide and she sprang up from the chair as though she'd been shocked, simultaneously screaming. The sound pierced the forest.

Tony stepped backward, moving his arms into a slow-down

19

motion.

"I'm sorry," he said loudly, unsure if she could hear him over the music. "I'm—"

"Who the hell are you?" she interrupted, yanking the earbuds from her ears. "This is private property."

"I'm sorry," he repeated. "I'm Tony. Tony Bradford. I got turned around up on the mountain and am trying to get back to town."

She eyed him suspiciously. "How do I know you're not some serial killer?"

"I promise, I'm not. I'm a minister."

"A minister?" She smoothed down her rumpled clothing, tugging her wrinkled shorts further down her legs. "Oh, sure," she said. "Sounds like something a serial killer would say." But she smiled fleetingly, as though acknowledging her paranoia.

She was tall and blonde with quick, sharp eyes that looked as though they didn't miss a thing. Her face was on the narrow side, the proportions imperfect enough that she wouldn't be a model. But she was striking just the same. Her voice was surprisingly deep and throaty. She caught Tony's eye and he felt heat climb up his neck, this time not due to the hot sun.

"This is a beautiful spot. Have you lived here long?" He glanced around the small yard.

She hesitated. Then, "No. No, I'm just visiting. For the summer."

Her stance was still wary, back stiff and straight as though waiting for Tony to launch himself at her in a homicidal frenzy. City dweller. New York, he'd guess by the slight accent.

"Me too. I've been here almost a week but keep getting lost." He chuckled. "I'm visiting too, from Boston. But I grew up here. In Vermont I mean. I've been away a long time."

She nodded stiffly. "I'm from New York."

"Again, sorry to startle you. I came up the driveway," he nodded back toward the long drive, "and thought you'd heard me on the gravel."

"Well, I didn't," she said and glanced around her, at the woods her gaze lingering by a little grove of three pine trees tightly packed together. He saw something cross her face, some emotion, but it was gone before he could place it.

She looked him up and down next, as though trying to figure something out. Then she sighed and shook her head.

"Sorry, I left my manners behind in the city, I guess. Can I get you something to drink?"

"I'd love some cold water."

"Sure." She crossed the porch to the door. Tony stayed planted where he was.

"You can come in if you like. Just don't judge me. I only got in yesterday and haven't finished unpacking yet."

"That's all right. I'll just sit here on the step."

She nodded and retreated into the house. Tony couldn't help but notice how long and toned her legs were as she walked past. He surveyed a bumblebee flying drunkenly out of a nearby flowerpot, trying to distract himself.

The woman—Tony realized now he didn't even know her name—had left the front door cracked. "Have you visited before?" he called out. Water ran inside.

"No, it's my first time in Stillwater," she called back. "First time to Vermont even." Then, "You?"

"I've never been this far north before."

Seconds later, she reappeared with a glass of water in hand. "I think the ice might be stale, so I just got the water as cold as possible." She handed the sweating glass over to him as he

21

stood.

He took several big gulps. "Thanks." Then, "I'm sorry, I didn't get your name."

"Oh. It's…Jessica. Jessica Brown."

He wondered about the pause, and she answered his unasked question. "Sorry. I write under a pen name and half the time can't remember which is my real one."

"You're an author?"

She nodded, but it seemed reluctant.

"What do you write?" Tony asked, draining the last of the water.

Jessica smiled slightly but wouldn't make eye contact. "Nothing you'd have read."

"Ah," Tony replied. "Erotica?" He grinned.

"No." She laughed as they made eye contact. Neither of them broke the gaze.

"It's romance," she said finally, then looked down, flicking a bug off her leg. "But please, don't tell anyone that I'm an author. I came here to get away from that—the media, the distractions, the noise. I don't want anyone here to know what I do for a living or who I am, so if you'd just keep it to yourself…" her voice drifted off.

"Sure, I get it. I'm here on a sort of sabbatical too."

"From preaching?"

"No, I'm not really a preacher."

"But you said—"

"I said I was a minister. There's a difference."

"Really?" She sounded skeptical. "What is it?"

"Well, I'm more of a spiritual guide," he paused, and she raised her eyebrows.

"Hmmm, too woo-woo?"

22

She nodded.

"I guess the best way to describe it is to say that I work with Christian CEOs and executives and help them to figure out what to do in certain circumstances. Help them to clarify what they've heard—or think they've heard—from God."

"So, you're like a Christian psychic?" Jessica's face was deadpan.

Was she joking? He couldn't tell. His job did sound weird, and he wasn't doing a great job of explaining it. "Not exactly," he shook his head. "Pastors are responsible for a single church—for one group of people. But I go into a business, sit with the leaders and try to figure out what steps they need to take to follow God's will for their organization."

"Ah," Jessica said, "I see."

Her voice said she didn't, but Tony let it go.

"So, I guess we're both sort of hiding out up here, huh?" He wanted to ask her for another glass of water but didn't.

"Looks like it," she agreed. They were quiet for several seconds, the drone of the bumblebee and the renewed chatter of birds, and one especially noisy squirrel overhead filled in the quiet.

"Did you know there is some sort of big festival going on soon?" Jessica asked.

"Oh, uh, yeah. I did know about that." Tony felt betrayed by the heat that climbed up his neck. She looked at him curiously, so he looked at the sky, the sun blinding him.

"Wait a minute," Jessica drew a step closer and peered up at him. It wasn't an unusual feeling. At nearly six foot five, Tony was used to looking down toward people. But what he wasn't used to was the way her eyes pinned him to the spot. And she was close. Closer than he'd realized. Her eyes were an unusual

23

gray color and rimmed with dark gold bands.

"Is that why you came here? To Stillwater?"

Tony shrugged and hoped it looked nonchalant.

"I might be a little interested in the gargun," he said.

"You've heard of it?" Now she looked incredulous.

"I told you I'm from here. Well, not here, here—not Stillwater, but down in the southern part of the state. I've been interested in these stories since back when I was a kid. Along with Champ in Lake Champlain and Bigfoot and all the rest."

"The rest? You mean there are more monsters in Vermont?" She cursed softly then glanced at him. "Sorry."

Tony laughed. "You hadn't heard? The state is rife with all kinds of monsters—everything from giant snakes and bats to shape shifters and big, hairy men—"

"I saw some of those driving through town yesterday," Jessica said.

Tony laughed again. It felt good: standing in the sun, a cool breeze just teasing his neck, less thirsty than he'd been ten minutes before. *And a beautiful companion to talk to*…the little voice in his head whispered, but he shrugged that thought away, guilt twisting in his belly. He had a beautiful companion back home. And just because things with Meredith had well, cooled, didn't mean that they weren't going to be together. That's what this little break was all about. She'd been unhappy with the idea at first, but they'd both decided it would be good for them. They both wanted to be sure they were the perfect partners everyone said they were.

"So, what's the deal?" Jessica raised one eyebrow.

For an unnerving second, Tony felt like she'd read his mind. He blinked, trying to remember where they'd been in the conversation.

"With the gargun." Her gaze strayed once again toward the little knot of pine trees. "People don't really believe in it, do they?"

Tony was relieved to think of something other than his love life. "Sure. Some of them, anyway. I've done a little," he cleared his throat, felt uncomfortable again. "A little research and there are some interesting signs that something—gargun or something else—lives in the lake here. There have been too many sightings over the years to just write it off as a bunch of fanatics."

Jessica squinted at him and shook her head, but she was smiling.

"A little research?"

Tony rubbed a hand over the back of his neck, the surface of his skin gritty from the dried sweat.

"Are you sure you're not one of those fanatics?"

"Well, maybe more than a little research," he admitted. "Since you told me one of your secrets, I'll tell you one of mine."

Jessica's lips curved upward, and Tony ignored his stomach flipping.

"I want to write a book about the gargun. I've been collecting information for years. But don't worry," he motioned with her hands that she should remain calm. "I'm not one of the out-there fanatics."

"Just a regular old one?"

Tony laughed. "Yeah. That kind."

They were quiet for a few seconds. Tony knew he should excuse himself but didn't want to.

"That was some storm last night." He'd resorted to talking about the weather. Pathetic.

"Yeah," Jessica glanced toward the upper level of her cabin.

"Something hit the house pretty hard. That window," she pointed to the one on the far left. "I forgot about it until just now." She wandered in that direction. "Any damage where you're staying?"

"No," Tony fell into step beside her.

"Oh, look," Jessica pointed at something in the grass. "Poor thing."

A blackbird, its neck broken, lay between a bush and the lawn. Tony glanced upward. There was a smudge in the window.

"That must be where he hit it," he pointed to the spot. Jessica followed his finger and nodded.

"I should bury it," she said. "Poor thing," she said again, stooping to look more closely at it. "It startled me. I was standing near the window and heard this loud bang."

Tony moved to the small shed. "I'll see if you have a shovel and take care of it."

"That's all right," Jessica stood but stayed where she was. "I can do that."

"It's no problem. I mean unless you're offended by a man helping you."

She laughed. "In this case, I'll let my feminist ideals slide."

He nearly stepped on a second dead crow minutes later, then found a third a few feet from that one.

"Uh, you might want to take a look at this," he called. Jessica joined him, eyes round.

"What happened?" she asked.

"I'm not sure. It's strange for birds to be out at night. Something must have scared them from their roosts."

"What did these hit?" She glanced around them. "Maybe the shed?"

The birds lay at least three yards from the small building.

Tony doubted they would have been thrown back that far but nodded.

"Yeah, maybe."

He found a shiny shovel in the shed, dug a big hole by the line of trees where the woods began and added each of the three birds. Their feet, wings, and shiny black eyes tumbled over one another into the hole, despite his best intention to place them in gently.

After covering them, he returned the shovel and they walked back to the little porch.

"I should get going. You probably have unpacking and other stuff to do." He handed Jessica back the glass from earlier. "Thanks for the water."

When their fingers touched on the glass, a jolt ran up his hand and arm. He glanced away, rearranged his feet. He felt suddenly as clumsy and awkward as he had in middle school: his feet too big, his sweaty shirt sticking to him. He didn't smell, did he? He wanted to lift an arm to check but didn't.

"Well. Thanks again." He retreated down the steps.

"Thank you," she said. "For taking care of those birds. And promising to not give away my secret about the author thing." Then, "Aren't you going to ask me?"

His heart did a single jumping jack in his chest.

"Ask you what?"

"You know. About how you can get published. If I can read your manuscript or put you in touch with a great agent?"

He shook his head, a half-smile on his face. "Do you get that a lot?"

"Just about all the time." She leaned against the porch's railing. "As soon as people hear you're an author, they want to tell you about their great idea for a book you should write. Or they

27

want you to read their great Aunt Tessie's memoir and pass it along to your agent."

She was funny, Tony thought. Funny and attractive and sharp. And he and Meredith were only taking a break, he reminded himself.

"Don't worry. I don't want you to read my book or connect me with anyone. I've only written a handful of chapters anyway. And they're not good."

She smiled. "Well, if you decided you wanted to tell me more about it, or about the gargun—just for fun—I wouldn't mind. It would break up the isolation of this place." She glanced back to the freshly turned soil.

"Sure," he said. Then added, "Actually, if you're interested, there's going to be a gargun talk at the historical society in town. It's at three. Maybe I'll see you there?"

"Sounds fun. Yes, I'll see you there. I'll be ready for another break by then."

Tony smiled, turned, and started down the driveway.

He should feel relieved. He knew exactly where the trail led, back to town. Instead, he felt a strange uneasiness beneath his skin, like something was crawling there. He glanced back, saw the little cabin growing smaller. Jessica had retreated inside, closed the front door behind her. But there was movement in an upper window. Maybe she'd run upstairs to retrieve something after going inside? A dark shape loomed in the clear glass, and stared out toward Tony. Or was it a trick of the light? He blinked and the shape was gone. He shook his head and jogged downhill.

Chapter 4

Vic Mellin

Victor sighed and hoped it would get his point across.

They'd been in this meeting for what felt like hours. The mayor's office was small and too hot, and someone hadn't remembered their deodorant. Glancing around surreptitiously, Vic noted that he wasn't the only one getting antsy. The doctor—Melanie? Melissa?—was jiggling her right foot on her left knee. Up, down, up, down, up, down. It made Vic feel dizzy and he looked away. The sheriff, who the mayor referred to as Rinko—Vic wasn't sure if that was a first or last name—stifled a yawn. The mayor's secretary, who appeared to be about twelve, watched the path of a trapped fly in the window with rapt attention. Her notebook balanced on her knee wobbled precariously and she shifted, gripping it more securely without changing the direction of her gaze.

"Just so we're on the same page," the mayor said for the millionth time since the little group of people had been seated. "I want to make sure that everything goes off without a hitch. We've run this festival successfully for the past forty-nine years and I want this year to go better than ever before."

He glanced around the little group.

"Sheriff, I know you deputize a few locals for the event."

Rinko sat straighter in his seat and made his eyes open too wide, as though forcing himself awake. It gave him a comical, cartoonish look: the bulging blue eyes popping out of the lined, permanently suntanned face. It sported a toothbrush-bristle mustache so thick it flared upwards where it had been recently trimmed.

"I do. I've already spoken to the three gentlemen and one lady who will be serving at the festival," Rinko replied. "They've all volunteered before. Got a training session scheduled for tomorrow evening. We'll do a few drills to be ready for Friday night."

"Good," Mayor Bloomberg replied, and Vic waited for him to add in the standard, "just so we're on the same page," but he didn't.

"And Melanie," he glanced toward the physician who didn't still her foot. "You're all set as far as the First Aid tent?"

"Yup." She rose to her feet. "And I'm sorry, Mayor Bloomberg, but I have to run. I have a ten o'clock appointment and the rest of the day is packed with patients. If there's anything I miss, will you send me the notes?" She glanced at the receptionist who, startled out of her reverie, looked back and forth between the doctor and mayor a couple of times.

"Of course," the mayor replied on her behalf. "Thanks for your time today."

"Sure, no problem," Melanie said. She looked around the room and nodded at everyone, gave a halfhearted wave, and let herself out of the stuffy space. A breath of slightly-less stale air filled the space when the door opened.

Vic stood up too.

"Mr. Mayor, I need to continue with my scouting work as

30

well. I appreciate you including me in this meeting though." Vic lied easily and followed it up with his camera-ready grin. The mayor smiled back, and the sheriff shifted again in his chair. His eyes had already returned to half-mast.

"Of course," the mayor responded. "Becky will get you the minutes for the meeting. And I'd just like to reiterate how important this piece you're doing is to our little community. The truth is that without this festival, Stillwater would really be hurting financially. Not that we're in great shape as it is," he sighed, puffing out his cheeks. "But we'd be much worse off. We're very pleased that you've chosen our humble town as a location for the show."

Vic nodded and kept the megawatt smile on his face.

"Happy to be here," Vic replied. "And I'm sure that this segment will bring interest and hopefully more tourists to the area. I do have to warn you though that there are no guarantees. This is a beautiful, remote location. But its remoteness works against it too, as a tourist draw, as I'm sure you're aware. People like to get out in the woods, but when they have a chance of a wilderness-like experience and the real thing? Well, most often they choose the sugar-coated version."

"But," the mayor blustered, his loud voice causing Rinko to flinch and jerk to alertness. "Surely the gargun is a draw. You said yourself that the evidence of something here in our lake is good."

Vic shifted his weight. "I believe it is. And once I get the film crew up here, we're going to do the very best job we can to capture the creature on film and promote your little town right along with it."

Mayor Bloomberg nodded in agreement, and then stood and leaned across his battered old desk to shake hands. Vic turned and shook hands with the sheriff and Becky, who looked slightly startled to be included.

Vic retreated from the office. The air on Main Street wasn't a lot cooler but it was certainly fresher. He'd noticed driving into town a couple of days before how good the air smelled: the perfect blend of pine and that hard-to-describe loamy scent of the earth in a forest. It reminded him of his childhood.

Still, the little walk down memory lane was about all he'd enjoyed being out here in no man's land. The cell signal was terrible, there were bugs and grubs, no Starbucks or other decent coffee to be found, and virtually no entertainment. The town pool was only a little larger than some of the larger Jacuzzis he'd spent time in, and a sad-looking movie theater featured movies from months ago. He hadn't even seen a decent-looking bar yet, only a rundown-looking biker place he'd been too intimidated to set foot in.

But look on the bright side, Vic thought. Without distractions, he'd have an opportunity to scout the perfect filming spots. Was it unusual for the star of the show to do prep location work? Sure, but Vic liked to keep his spoon in the pot, as his grandma used to say. He wanted to know every option: which landscape would cast him in the best light, which backdrop would highlight his features, which lighting would best hide the fine wrinkles around his eyes and mouth. That and the fact that he always had to keep his eye on the bottom line now. The film crew he'd told the mayor about consisted of his producer, Nikki, and her younger brother, Joe, who was a production assistant and cameraman both.

A big logging truck rumbled down the street, loaded with thick trees denuded of branches. Vic had once dated a woman—a beautiful, sexy creature—who'd been so into the environmental movement that she and a band of her friends had strapped themselves to old trees. They'd refused to move for days. But then she'd been offered a bit role in a Hollywood production and had forgotten the trees.

Growing up in British Columbia, Vic had learned the hard way that nature wasn't always pretty and cooperative. He'd lived in the city for years now—since leaving home at seventeen in fact—and had never regretted his decision. Growing up in a big farming family, Vic had never fit in. While his siblings had all dreamed of having their own farm-related businesses one day, or of taking over the family's dairy farm, Vic couldn't think of anything worse than getting stuck in their tiny rural town. He'd dreamed of being an actor and thought he had a good chance of making it. Unfortunately, casting directors didn't agree, and he'd found himself like hundreds of other wannabes: waiting tables or making drinks behind a bar. Still, if it wasn't for his rural beginnings, he'd never have started this film company.

He and his best friend, Guy, had dreamed about it for years. They'd discussed every possible situation on long backpacking trips, then taken all of that and eventually gotten it down on paper. They'd wanted to hit it big—NOVA, National Geographic TV, or other documentary companies would be calling them, maybe even fighting over the rights to their documentaries.

Neither of them had realized how much capital it would take to get their dream off the ground. The proudest moment of Vic's life had been signing the final partnership paperwork at the lawyer's office, making Backyard Films official.

"Here's to shoot out of the filmmaking industry like a rocket," Guy had toasted him that night over beers at Verdugo.

But they hadn't anticipated how long liftoff would take.

Weeks turned into months, and months into years and still they were filling the schedule book with bread-and-butter gigs: filming weddings and bar mitzvahs and one-off projects for graphic designers who needed promotional videos for clients. They kept all this work separate from Backyard Films, of course. Didn't want to taint their art and future glory with the grunt work that paid the bills. "It's just around the corner," they kept telling each other as they continued hustling on their dream.

And then three months ago, Guy had let his half of the rocket tip unceremoniously off the launch pad. Over a craft beer, he'd told Vic that he wanted out. Then, despite Vic's loud protests and cajoling, Guy had cashed in on his half of the company. Vic had known Guy hadn't been happy—he certainly hadn't hidden his disbelief over the way the company was going through its reserves—but Vic hadn't expected his oldest friend to leave him in the lurch.

"We're almost there, man," he'd tried to reason with Guy who was cleaning out his half of their shared office. "You can't give up now."

Guy had only snorted and kept tossing things into his nylon duffle bag.

"Wake up, Vic," Guy had leaned against the doorframe. "It's never going to happen."

Now, Vic was committed to making Backyard Films a success, no matter what. He wasn't ashamed to admit that he fantasized about future glory and the way he'd shove it in Guy's face when the company accepted its first indie film award. He pictured the scenario when things were especially tough and each time it was a little sweeter.

Was the film company struggling financially? Sure. But this trip, this location would change all of that. When the crew got a shot of the gargun it would change everything. The footage would go viral and then the film company's ranking would skyrocket, blasting up to the upper echelon ranks of Vimeo and YouTube, and other media platforms. Not to mention what it would do for Backyard Films' reputation. Vic had been envisioning the phone calls and email requests pouring in: maybe one of the Discovery or History channels hunting them down to ask them for a contract. That would be a welcome change to what had become a major part of Vic's work life: putting the film company's work out there and begging for a simple look. Crowdfunding and begging and borrowing to keep the business afloat.

He slid behind the steering wheel of the battered white company van, made sure all the windows were down. He'd go back to the lake. He'd been mapping out the areas where the gargun had historically been spotted. Unfortunately, the sightings weren't consistent. Summertime though seemed to be the most popular time of the year for the gargun to make an appearance. Maybe it would highlight its own festival, Vic thought. Today, he'd get in the water, check for potential underwater shots and determine where the light and angle would be best. He used to employ someone to do this work for him, but the budget-slashing he'd done recently meant he was back to doing things the old way—by himself. And that was okay with Vic. Nikki and Joe would have the final say of course. For the paltry salaries he paid them, their final direction and promise of names in the credits were non-negotiable.

He slowed to a crawl while following the narrow, steep road down to the lake which lay before Vic, shining and blue as a sapphire. When it gave up its secrets about the gargun, Vic would be rolling in those jewels and a lot of other expensive things soon.

Chapter 5

Sheriff Robert Rinko

Rinko went for a cup of coffee and a slice of pie at Betsy's after the meeting at the mayor's office. Betsy's niece, whose name he rarely remembered, knew to make his coffee extra strong. She kept a pot on the back burner of the multi-pot unit, hot and ready for him.

"Thanks," he said as Suzie—her nametag reminded him—refilled his cup. He drank it black and as usual, didn't wait long enough for that first sip, burning the tip of his tongue in the process.

The diner was nearly empty this afternoon. The lunch crowd would have already cleared out. A wealthy-looking couple sat hunched over a map at a table closest to the door. They had on outdoor gear, so new that it practically glowed.

"I don't think it's a good idea," the man was saying. "These are unfamiliar trails, Barbara. It's not like back home."

The woman started shaking her head before he'd even finished speaking.

"Don't be such a baby. This is why we came here, isn't it? To challenge ourselves." Her voice was thickly laced with disgust. "Imagine what our friends will say when we get back if we came all this way and didn't climb it?"

Rinko swirled a spoon unnecessarily through his coffee and took another bite of pie. It was two-thirty in the afternoon, too early to be eating dessert. But the pie was lemon so technically, he was eating fruit. And the crust wasn't much different than toast, right? True, he'd already inhaled a twelve-inch sub at his desk earlier, but…

Rinko popped another bite of pie in. The sweet and tart stickiness was exactly what he needed to wake him up. That and a refill on the dark coffee.

"…just don't think it's a good idea," the man was saying again. He shook his head. Rinko could see a little bald shiny spot underneath the man's thinning hair that had been carefully combed to hide it.

Rinko thought about going over there. Help settle the peace, and aid the couple in some sort of logical compromise. But he was too tired. He would be sixty-eight next month, too old to be sheriff, some would say. He certainly didn't have the vim and vigor he had as a young officer. But Rinko was far from pushing up daisies. He had at least one more year in him, he figured. Then his pension would be nearly three times what it was five years ago.

"You're just coasting now," Marie said to him more than once. "Waiting it out. You'd better hope nothing big happens."

"That's the beauty of this place, Marie," Rinko had replied. "Nothing big ever happens in Stillwater." And it was true. Other than the yearly festival—which to be honest had been the highlight of his year for the many he'd been in charge—there was little need for a full-time sheriff to be employed. Sure, he had the occasional drunk and disorderly (usually Norm Webster) and the occasional domestic abuse reports (normally

Sarah Peters, who never wanted to press charges and had a mean left hook of her own). Other than that, life in Stillwater was calm. And Rinko liked it that way.

Course, there was an influx of visitors-turned-residents in the past few years. Even though the town itself looked more and more neglected, tourists who came for the gargun festival, hiking, or Nordic skiing in winter, decided that a one- or two-week visit wasn't enough. That had been why Rinko's office had finally gotten approval for a part-time deputy.

Marie was right though. Rinko was coasting now. Just twelve more months—eleven if he cashed in all his unused vacation time—and he'd be home free. He and Marie had been making retirement plans. Unfortunately, neither of them wanted to do the same things. Rinko dreamed of heading out on an epic fly-fishing trip, one that lasted most of the next summer. Marie, on the other hand, wanted to do a road trip to visit her one remaining sister in Wisconsin. Rinko couldn't think of anything he'd rather do less.

"…being ridiculous! If you're too much of a coward, I'll go on my own!" the woman's voice cut through Rinko's thoughts, jarred him back to the present. He looked up from his empty plate in time to see the well-dressed woman storm from the café. The man, her husband or boyfriend, sighed and started to gather up the map. He signaled to Suzie who rushed to get his bill for him.

Poor bugger, Rinko thought. Marie could be hard-headed at times (she preferred the term "persistent") but at least she never resorted to name-calling, no matter how mad she got. Rinko hefted himself from the booth and walked to the man's table cradling his mug of still-too-hot coffee. The man looked up. He was thin and lanky, with little round dark-rimmed glasses.

39

He had the look that many of the tourists up here arrived with: like their bodies held onto the stress of the cities they'd fled from. Shoulders up around their ears, backs so straight they looked like they wore braces under their clothes, eyes darting here and there with nervous energy.

"Robert Rinko," the sheriff held out his hand.

"Rubin Vander." The man's hand was cool, and the tendons were strong and ropy. Rinko had expected something limpid.

"Going hiking?" Rinko asked and took a sip of his coffee.

"Yes, hiking is on the docket," Vander said. "Unfortunately, my wife is under the impression that we're true mountaineers as well as in our twenties." He smiled grimly.

Rinko chuckled politely. "That does sound like a challenge."

Pause. Another sip of coffee. Then, "Where are you thinking of going?"

"She wants to try Elmer's Point," Vander said. He struggled to get the map folded back the way it had been. "I don't think it's a good idea, especially as it's our first hike in Vermont. It's our first time in Stillwater," the man sounded almost apologetic.

Rinko made a noncommittal noise. He wanted to fold the map himself but let the man struggle on. A gold Rolex glinted on the man's wrist and his shirt still had that new-off-the-hanger crispness to it.

"Well, now. Elmer's Point is a difficult trail. But you might enjoy the summit at Philomena. It's close to Elmer's, but the terrain isn't as challenging. Don't get me wrong," Rinko held up his hand and made a "stop" motion. "It's still plenty difficult. But not as technically challenging as Elmer's. Not so many built-in ladders and such."

The man nodded and finally, frustrated with the map, wadded it up and stuck it under his arm. His cheeks were red and Rinko felt the irritation radiate from him.

"Yeah, thanks, Sheriff. We may do that. If I can convince Barbara, that is."

"Does she have her own map?" Rinko asked.

The man shook his head. "She's not good with maps. We've taken a couple of different orienteering classes, but for some reason, it just hasn't clicked. We usually use a GPS but that doesn't work around here we discovered yesterday."

"Then there you go," Rinko gave the man a wink. "You tell her you're doing Elmer's Point. Signage at the trailhead includes both—the trails split off later. By that time, she might be seeing things more from your point of view."

Vander smiled, his thin lips nearly disappearing as he did so. "Sheriff, I like the way you think."

Rinko shrugged. "It's all in the day's work, Mr. Vander."

"Rubin, please. And thanks for your help."

Rinko nodded. "You have yourselves a good trip. Looks to be a beautiful day."

Rinko decided to forgo the second cup of coffee, his tongue still tender from the burn the first had given him. He left Suzie a three-dollar tip beside his empty mug.

What to do with the rest of the afternoon? Doug would be starting his shift shortly, but Rinko still had a couple of hours to kill. Patrolling the streets held no interest. There was a list of things his office had to do for the upcoming festival but the sheriff's department's office manager, Billie Jo, handled all that and doled out necessary tasks. She always cut Rinko slack, made sure to give most of the grunt work to Doug and the volunteer deputies that the office utilized during the festival.

Billie Jo and Rinko had been with the sheriff's office the same number of years, but she still referred to him jokingly as "the new guy," seeing as she'd started six months before him. Back then, Billie Jo had been a young girl learning the ropes in dispatch, and Rinko, a strong buck, was the greenest of the deputies. As well as the only one. Old Sheriff Thompson had gotten the cancer diagnosis early enough to train Rinko, but not nearly enough to give the older man a fighting chance.

Rinko rubbed a hand over his face, felt the skin tighten under it before it went slack again. A glance in the rearview mirror showed him the same old face which still surprised him. Where had the lines come from and the hair gone? At least his mustache hadn't lost any of its girth.

Swinging the cruiser around in a gentle arc, Rinko headed toward Stillwater Lake. Maybe he'd check up on their out-of-town guest, Victor Mellin, and see if he could offer any expertise. He'd mentioned he would be scouting the area and Rinko had mentioned the lake as the natural place to begin. The gargun was a funny thing: half the town was dead set on believing it was real, and the other half considered it along the same lines as aliens and Bigfoot. Fun tales to tell around a campfire but without any real merit.

The cruiser swept across town, Rinko raising his hand in a friendly wave to a few shopkeepers, the mayor's wife, and the local pastor as he cut across the side streets and onto the main drag. The road there was deserted now but when the festival started it would be bumper-to-bumper traffic and hordes of people. Now, the lake like a giant bowl of blue-green glass was visible to Rinko's right.

His hands tightened slightly on the wheel like they always did on this stretch. The road was too narrow to catch a glimpse of the beach and boat launch area, further down. The gears on the old Ford ground slightly as Rinko made it through the pass—a skinny stretch of road that ran through the mountains on one side and the steep drop over a ravine to Gargun's Footstool, on the other. He always found himself holding his breath when he passed through here. The old rhyme he'd learned as a kid stuck deep in his subconscious.

Don't you breathe and don't you blink,
  The gargun's standing at his sink.
  Washing blood from every blade,
  To cut you for each sin you've made.
  Don't get close and don't look down,
  He'll follow you right back to town.
  Tucked so safely in your bed,
  The gargun will find you...

Now, what was the last word? Rinko paused, his foot automatically lessening on the gas pedal. The car began to crawl up the hill and he overcorrected and applied too much pressure. The old sedan shot forward. The tires skittered on the loose stone of the road.

He looked nervously toward the edge of the ravine. What had once been a proper guardrail, was now a rusted and sagging section of bent metal. Years of moisture, heavy snows, and salt had done their work. The town had been putting off replacing it because of the new snowplow it had had to purchase last year.

Rinko grimaced and slammed his foot on the brake. The pedal sank halfway to the floor, spongy and soft. The car continued to skid, as though on a sheet of ice. The tires weren't new and didn't have enough traction on the pebbled road.

Rinko swore and jerked upward on the emergency brake. Then he saw something. He squinted, tried to make out the shadow from the rock. He blinked, mouth open. That couldn't be. It couldn't—Rinko heard a yell. Realized with surprise it had come from his open mouth. The car bucked. His hands scrabbled over the wheel twisting and pulling. He slammed his foot on the useless brake again.

Rinko stared mutely with horror. The car ran at the shadowy shape as though pulled like a magnet.

Rinko had to get out.

Had to jump.

His hand fumbled with the handle, but the door wouldn't budge.

It was too late.

The car sailed forward. Over the scrubby undergrowth and saplings and the rocky bank of the ravine. Trees and vines and dark earth and black stone rushed past Rinko so fast that he felt dizzy. He held his breath. An image of Marie that morning came to mind. She'd been sitting at the kitchen table her long braid over one shoulder of her robe, her favorite bluebird mug in one hand. She turned toward him, mouth opened wide in a scream.

Just before the impact, Rinko remembered the last line of the poem.

The gargun will find you; make you wish you were dead.

Chapter 6

Vic Mellin

Vic pulled off his flippers on the damp, slippery old dock that jutted out into the lake. He surveyed the area. It wasn't a good place for a dock. Some big, old trees with low-hanging branches made a canopy over it, preventing the sun from penetrating their foliage. That in turn made the wood slick with algae and a thin layer of moss.

He shook his head, discouraged. The water itself wasn't as clear as he'd hoped. It was filled with bits of algae—some brownish sort—which would make underwater shots extremely hard to make. But further out maybe, it would be better. And the beach at least was in good shape. There were mountains around every side of the lake, making it look like a blue bowl. He was surprised the water didn't appear brown but the sky overhead—a pure, vibrant blue—must be helping in that regard.

The sun was hot but welcome as Vic gathered his equipment and headed for a large, smooth boulder. He sat on it, the sun warming his skin and drying the wetsuit he'd pulled off.

He rolled his shoulders a few times, heard his neck pop when he stretched his head from side to side. It was strange how just a couple of days out here in the wilderness had helped him slow down. He didn't feel any utopian peacefulness per se, but it did seem like the slower pace of life here was having some effect. He'd have to be careful that it didn't get out of control. He was on a deadline and every day here was costing him money. Once Nikki and Joe arrived, that meant more out-of-pocket expenses. He had to remain clear, focused. Vic referred to his mental checklist of things to do.

First, he'd need to—

A huge explosion jerked Vic upward on the rock. To his far right, a fireball erupted in the sky followed nearly immediately by a dark gray cloud of smoke. His mouth hung open and for a moment, he questioned what he was seeing. It looked so much like a movie set—the perfect mushroom cloud of smoke, the blaze in the valley down below.

It was the smell of smoke that jerked him from his inertia. Vic jumped up, pulled on his sneakers, and started to run toward the smoke. About fifty paces in he stopped. This was something worth filming. He sprinted back to his pile of stuff, rooted around in his bag, and found the small DSLR camera, then sprinted back toward the smoke. He could call for help, only his cellphone didn't get a signal. Should he run to town instead?

But what if someone survived the crash—even as he thought it, Vic knew it wasn't true. Not unless whoever it was had bailed out of the car or plane or whatever the vehicle was before impact.

A car. It had to be. He'd have heard a plane, even a small one. His legs burned and his lungs ached. He cursed himself for all the times he'd made excuses rather than going to the gym and pulled himself over boulders and smaller stones. He went slowly enough to not roll an ankle but fast enough to get to the burning debris as quickly as he could. The brush was thick and choking. In places, he had to slow to a walk, through the vines and thick bunches of prickly thorn bushes. He skirted trees and nearly fell once as his feet skittered on the loose stones nearer the lake. Here, the land hadn't been trained into a beachfront. The wildness of vegetation butted right up to the water. Vic could see the lake, sparkling and beckoning to his left. He continued; his breathing ragged in the now-still air.

Suddenly, the dense foliage emptied into a rocky, craggy stretch of land. Ahead maybe two hundred yards was a burning wreck of metal and plastic. He choked on the thick smoke before he could draw close enough to see if there was anyone inside. The vehicle—a car—had landed on its top. It was completely caved in. One tire was still slowly spinning but the car was a mass of flames. Vic had to stop twenty or thirty yards away. The heat was like a hand that slammed him backward. He bent over, hands on knees, gasping for air, coughing on smoke.

What had happened? He looked up. Far, far above he could see a rusted guardrail. It bordered the road Vic had driven over an hour or so earlier. He remembered the stretch. He'd clenched both hands on the steering wheel and slowed to a crawl.

Maybe this poor guy had taken it too fast. Maybe it was another tourist, like Vic, who hadn't realized the danger. They'd overlooked the signs warning of a narrow road and steep drop.

Vic pulled the small, expensive camera from his pocket and started to record. He wasn't sure why he'd need this footage, but it didn't hurt to document it. He filmed the blazing car, the smoke drifting upward, and then traced a path from the vehicle to the road above. At one point as the camera's viewfinder slid over the stone wall of the ravine, Vic thought he saw something moving across the rock face. But when he tried to find the spot again, he couldn't.

The sun was hot on his back and a trickle of sweat crept from his hairline down the back of his neck.

"...okay?"

A voice echoed down through the ravine, barely audible over the blaze of the flames. Vic flicked the camera off and looked up toward the road above him. No one there. Then he saw movement to his left, far down on the barren stretch. An area between the car and whatever land lay beyond it. More woods, it looked like. A figure waved its arms.

"Are...okay? Get...help?" The voice called. Female.

"Yes!" Vic yelled back. "Go get help!"

The figure hesitated a second, then turned. Vic suddenly realized he didn't want to be alone with this burning wreck and the poor dead soul trapped inside. Besides, if the woman was a local, she might know of a shortcut back to town. He skirted the fire, staying far enough away that he had to wade through the shallow water of the lake. The water was cold and his feet slipped and slid on the rocks despite his water shoes. He stumbled once and nearly fell before getting close enough to yell to the retreating figure.

"Wait!"

The woman stopped, turned.

Vic slogged out of the water and further down the barren landscape. The rock walls here were jagged and looked impossible to climb.

"Are you okay?" she called as he drew closer. Vic nodded, then realized she couldn't see him.

"Yes. It wasn't...it wasn't my car. Poor guy must have blown through that stretch too fast, come over the edge. I was further down, at the beach." Vic paused. "Is there a faster way back to town than the road?" He was close enough now to see the woman. She was attractive: tall and blonde with her hair drawn up in a ponytail. Her tanned, toned legs were in a pair of linen shorts.

"I—I don't know. I was just walking from my cabin. I think I took a wrong turn somewhere," she sounded sheepish. "I'm just visiting."

"Me too," Vic said. "Look, let's go back to my van. It's just over there, past the dock." He pointed behind him.

She hesitated, glanced behind her. Vic had been right: there was a thick forest beyond. She seemed to weigh something in her mind, then nodded.

"We'll drive to town and let them know what happened."

"What did happen?" She fell into step with him.

"Someone went over the edge of the ravine. I can't tell what type of vehicle it was other than it was a car. A sedan."

She put a hand to her open mouth. "Oh God, how awful. No survivors?"

He shook his head. "I don't think so. It's pretty bad."

Her long legs easily kept up with Vic's pace. He was used to walking with Nikki, who was all of five feet. She'd trained him to slow down so that she didn't have to trot everywhere.

"Maybe an animal ran out in front of them?"

Vic shook his head. "Maybe. But it's a bad stretch of road. Pretty dangerous. You haven't been out that way yet?"

The woman shook her head. "No, I just got here yesterday. This is my first exploration."

Vic held a branch out of the way as he passed by so that it wouldn't slap back in her face.

"I'm Victor Mellin, by the way," he said, "Vic. I'm with Backyard Films, here to do a documentary on the area."

"I'm Jessica Brown," she said. "I'm...I'm just here on vacation."

"Good to meet you. Though I wish it were under different circumstances."

She made a sympathetic noise.

They retraced Vic's earlier path, keeping their distance from the burning heap of metal. Jessica made a sound of distress as they skirted the accident scene. Eventually, they reached the boulder holding his stuff. He grabbed the towel, flippers, wetsuit, his underwater camera, and phone in its waterproof case, stuffed everything back into the fraying canvas bag. Jessica trailed him back to his vehicle, still parked near the dock.

"Hop in," he said.

She climbed in the passenger's side door as he tossed the bag into the back. Then he gunned the engine and reversed, headed back up to the road and the town beyond.

Chapter 7

Tony Bradford

Tony shifted on the hard folding chair in the cramped room. The Stillwater Historical Society appeared as ancient as the documents and photos it housed. The walls were covered in dark wainscoting, likely original to the building. The floors were scarred wooden planks that creaked underfoot. Folding chairs had been set too closely together facing a small podium made of heavy, dark wood. Black and white photos of town streets and solemn people lined the walls and the air smelled of coffee, old paper, and dust.

He'd expected the lecture to be popular, but not this popular. Jessica Brown hadn't shown up yet. Tony tried to ignore the disappointment that lay like a stone in his gut. She was still settling in, and it had likely slipped her mind. Anyway, he shouldn't have invited her to begin with. Would he want Meredith asking a man she didn't know to some event with her while he was away? Sure, they were taking a little time apart, but that didn't mean they weren't still together. At least, Tony had hoped it didn't.

It was one of the reasons that he'd come on this sabbatical. Yes, he needed the time away from work, which was a strange blend of satisfaction and stress. And yes, he was intrigued by the gargun. But, he shifted uncomfortably in his chair, there was another, smaller reason. He needed to figure out where he stood—where he wanted to stand—with Meredith. She'd made it clear that she wasn't going to wait for him forever. His foot-dragging was going to get him into trouble. In fact, it already had.

She was getting frustrated. Tony didn't blame her. On paper, Meredith was everything he'd ever wanted in a partner: she was smart and capable, a good conversationalist, and interesting. She had tons of energy and was always up to try new things. She was warm and friendly, loving. Committed in her relationship to God. She'd make a great mother...

So why was Tony still unsure about buying the ring? He'd tried to explain it to his father, but he'd ended up as frustrated with Tony as Meredith had been.

"Where will you ever find another woman as perfect for you as she is?" Dad had asked.

And Tony hadn't had a good answer. His mother had been more understanding.

"When it's the right person, you just know," she'd said. "You'll know."

"Good afternoon, ladies and gentlemen," a thin, reedy voice wavered from the podium. The murmur of the crowd quieted slowly.

"I'm happy to welcome you here to the Stillwater Historical Society's Annual Informational Session. I'm Haven Southport, the president of this organization. Today, we're pleased to welcome Joshua Gaven, a renowned expert on mythology, lore, and a born cryptozoologist." Murmurs started around the room again, but Haven continued to speak over them.

"Joshua hales from Minnesota originally—but we'll forgive him his flatlander status—" The crowd chuckled. "Please, let's give a warm welcome to him."

Applause filled the room and Tony took the opportunity to pull off the hiking vest he'd added earlier. The room was hot and the slow fans circling overhead were ineffective.

"Good afternoon," Joshua Gaven approached the podium and stood behind it easily. You could tell he's done this a few hundred times, Tony thought.

"Thank you, Ms. Southport, for the great introduction, and while it's true that I was born in Minnesota, my family spent summers in Vermont all during my childhood. I guess that still doesn't change my status but wanted to put that card on the table," Joshua chuckled and the crowd did too. It was an old joke—that transplants to the area were flatlanders for at least a couple of generations—but it always got a laugh. Tony had forgotten that dyed-in-the-wool pride that came from simply being a third or fourth or fifth-generation Vermonter in this hard climate.

Joshua was young, maybe in his early thirties, and sported a hipster vibe with snug jeans, a grizzly beard, and despite the heat, a little knitted beanie.

"I'm sure that you all could tell me a thing or two about the gargun that lives here in your lake."

Whispers and more chuckles sounded from around the room.

"And I'm certainly not here to preach to the choir." More chuckles.

"No, what I want to talk to you about today is the scientific research that's been done proving that there is indeed a creature—a very old, very elusive creature—living in Stillwater Lake."

"We know that," a loud man's voice called from the back of the room, "because we've seen him!"

Joshua nodded, smiled. "And did you get a picture?"

The man grunted a no.

"That's the problem—when we're looking for things like the gargun or other folk legends," he made air quotes with his fingers. "We very rarely have the camera ready. That's why it's been so difficult to prove that creatures such as Bigfoot exist. Now, we know," he emphasized the word, "we". "We know that that gargun is real. But what I'm here to share with you today is the technology that is going to allow us to not only verify that this creature is out there in your lake but what it looks like, where it came from, its age, its habits in and out of the water...things we've always wanted to know but could never grasp. That's what the newest technology is teaching us.

"For instance, going back to Bigfoot: did you know that there have been samples of hair found, which have been tested in the lab and verified as non-human and non-animal? At least, not any animal that biologists have ever seen before. Casts of footprints captured by people just like you and me have helped scientists to determine that there is more than one type of Bigfoot creature. So perhaps the Yeti and Sasquatch and Bigfoot are all distinct animals, with distinct DNA and similar but very different traits. That's the type of research that I want to do here in Stillwater.

"Getting that kind of data will help us—all of us—to really understand the gargun. What it wants. What it's doing here," Joshua spread his arms wide as if the gargun was sitting amongst them. "If there is more to its story than meets the eye. Now, what can you tell me historically, about the gargun?"

Joshua paused. At first, it was quiet in the room, the only

sounds that of groaning chairs as people shifted their weight and the whispered sound of brochures fanning hot faces. But then someone spoke up from the middle of the room.

"It's like the Scottish selkies," a woman said. "It's lived in the lake longer than any of us or even our great-grandparents have lived here. Comes up on land to feed every so often when the supply of fish runs low."

"I've heard that philosophy," Joshua smiled. "Anyone else?"

"It's part sea serpent and part man," another voice called.

"Nah, it's a cross between a crocodile and a human," said someone else.

"No, it ain't." A woman's voice rang out. "It's the devil himself come to life."

Heads swiveled toward the left of the room. A solidly built woman with short curls leaned against the wall.

"Now you've done it. Margie's all in a tizzy," a man called from the back of the room. Chuckles followed his statement.

But Joshua raised his eyebrows. "Well, that's a theory I've heard less about. Can you tell us more?"

The woman, Margie, glared and shook her head. She muttered something that sounded like "idiots" under her breath.

"People say that one of the founders of this town, Claude Johnson, made a pact with the devil," a well-modulated voice said from Tony's right. He glanced over and saw a man with thinning blondish hair and a long, patrician nose. His pressed khakis and a long-sleeve white dress shirt with the sleeves neatly rolled up were out of place. The rest of the room was filled with people dressed in shorts and tank tops, work pants, and T-shirts.

"That's a lie!" Margie broke in. "It wasn't Johnson, it was Briggs!"

"Hold on, hold on. Everyone who has valuable information to share will have a chance to contribute, I promise," Joshua said. "Please, go on mister...?

"I'm Harlan Knobb, a history professor-turned-innkeeper. I run Meadowlark Bed and Breakfast," Harlan smoothed a hand over his hair. "This is an old legend and not a very popular one. Most people don't like the idea of their kin being in league with the devil. The history is muddled of course, and there's nothing on paper that's ever been found. Just the belief that Johnson made a pact with the devil, as I said."

Murmurs from around the room, a few snorts of disbelief.

"Ah, not this again," the man from the back of the room said.

"Go on," Joshua said again, undeterred. "Tell us more."

Harlan waited a moment as though gathering his thoughts. Tony wondered if he'd rehearsed what he was about to say. He seemed pleased to have an audience.

"It's a story that's been handed down through generations, from grandfather to grandchild. The kind told on long summer evenings or cold wintery nights. Claude Johnson made a pact with the devil in exchange for success in his business."

"That's a load of bull," Margie glared at Harlan.

"We came here to hear the science." Back-of-the-room-man broke in. Then more quietly, "Not fairytales from the fairy."

Harlan, his cheeks pink, lifted his chin higher. "My family has lived here in Stillwater for several generations. We're descendants of Ethan Allen himself—"

"It wasn't Johnson that made that pact and you know it! Your family is the reason our town is cursed," Margie pointed a finger at Harlan. "You and your stupid—"

"Please, let's keep this civil, folks," Joshua interrupted.

"She's right. This is garbage," the man called. Tony craned his neck to see who was speaking but the crowd was too thick. "I came here to hear about that new technology, not a bunch of old wives' tales"

"We'll get there, sir," Joshua's voice was patient as he looked around the room. "We'll get there. But in every historical research process, you must first start with what you think you know about the subject being studied. Now, you may or may not believe in this historical recounting," Joshua's eyes swept the crowd, paused on Margie. "But the fact that it's been handed down over generations gives the story, if not weight, then at least an original perspective."

Margie growled under her breath but slouched back against the wall. The man in the back didn't say anything else as Joshua encouraged Harlan to continue. Tony was grateful. He'd never heard of the gargun having spiritual ties.

"This would have been back in the early 1800s, shortly after the state was formed in 1791," Harlan said, standing. His voice was louder than before. "There were only a handful of settlers here then. Claude Johnson and his friend, Jenson Briggs, started this town. They both had entrepreneurial spirits. Johnson in particular had big ideas. Like any serial entrepreneur will tell you, failure is just one part of long-term success. He'd had his share of bad luck and poor decisions. But starting over, here in northern Vermont, he was sure would solve his problems once and for all.

"He and his wife and their three sons along with Briggs and a few other families left city life behind to begin their own bourgeoise here in the country. They were all from wealthy families and pictured a place where they'd build a utopia of sorts. They planned to claim land, create a town, and make it and their families prosper."

The heat and crowded room around Tony faded as he listened. Harlan's well-modulated, rich voice was hypnotic.

"Only it didn't work out that way. While the families were all from New England, none of them had tried to make a living off the cold, hardscrabble land before. They were cut off from everything—family, friends, business connections—and started to feel the pinch. Briggs and Johnson planned to set up a logging operation and bring in more men to run it. They'd miscalculated the lake though, thought that the connection of it to rivers nearby would work for transporting the logs only to be disappointed. And the land was too rough, too untamed to transport logs by wagon.

"Briggs eventually found success, but Johnson never did. Until mysteriously—and the historical records don't show how—Johnson became mayor of Stillwater."

"His luck had changed," Joshua smiled.

Margie snorted loudly. "It didn't have anything to do with luck. Johnson was a hard worker, and a leader. That's why he became mayor. And why don't you tell him about Briggs? He didn't do too badly either, did he?"

Harlan cleared his throat. "Jenson Briggs did become a very wealthy man over time. He finally figured out a way to make the logging operation successful and started a lumber mill as well. He died a very rich man—"

"Because of the pact he made with the devil," Margie's curls trembled as she spoke. "Him, not Claude Johnson. My family would never be involved in something like that."

"It's wonderful that you want to protect your family's honor, Ms. Monteau," Harlan said.

"I wouldn't have to if you weren't so determined to drag it through the mud, Harlan." Margie said the man's name like it was laced with needles.

The room was so quiet a pencil dropping on the floor would have sounded like an explosion. Tony shifted in his seat.

"That's an interesting tale," Joshua said from the podium. "But I'm not quite sure how it fits in with the gargun."

"Because the gargun was birthed out of Briggs' pact," Margie said slowly as though explaining to a two-year-old. "That's how he became successful. He sold his soul—and our future—to darkness. No one knows exactly what the gargun is—how it works when it comes out of Stillwater Lake, but it always comes. Have you seen the reports? The newspaper articles? People go missing around here. People die in the lake or around it. That's the gargun."

"That's life, Margie," a woman from the back of the room called out. "People get lost. People die. It's just a fact of life."

Margie shook her head, gray curls swinging, then muttered something under her breath and stalked from the room letting the door slam behind her.

Whispers turned louder until they buzzed like bees drunkenly returning to a sun-warmed hive. Joshua plastered a smile on his face and glanced furtively at his watch.

"Well. Now that we have some of the lore behind the legend explained, let's look at some of the technology that I was talking about earlier," Joshua said, his clear voice cutting through the drone of voices. "I think it makes sense to—"

Suddenly, the door crashed open. Standing on the step and outlined by the brilliant sunshine stood a woman who looked vaguely familiar to Tony. Bright red curls spilled out of a ponytail and her cheeks were fire engine red. She owned the general store, he remembered.

"There's been an accident," she cried. "Sherriff Rinko went

over the cliff at Gargun's Footstool!"

Chapter 8

Lydia Donovan

"...and my sister said you could hear his screams all the way back to town."

Lydia shivered, her still-damp skin sprouting goosebumps. Alex must have noticed because he draped an arm casually over her shoulder. Lydia's insides went all squishy. They'd been talking about the accident, like everyone else in town.

"Really?" Lydia moved a couple of inches closer to Alex who smelled like leftover sunscreen and cologne and sunshine.

"Mmm," he said and slurped from the straw poking out of the tall paper cup. The straw sucked noisily at the bottom and Alex pitched the red cup with one smooth motion into the nearby trashcan. He was good at everything, Lydia realized.

"Point!" Kyle yelled from the other side of the picnic table and snickered. Katie was sitting stiffly next to him, trying to keep her distance. She widened her eyes at Lydia and made a slight motion with her head. *Let's go* her expression said. Lydia pressed her lips together and gave her puppy dog eyes. *Just a few more minutes?*

Katie, apparently getting the message, sighed loudly and started to swing her right foot under the table.

61

"I'm bored," she announced seconds later. "There's nothing to do around this place."

"We could go down to the lake. Check out the accident," Alex said.

"I don't think so, dummy," Katie said. "I doubt the police want people poking around there. They're probably like, collecting evidence and stuff."

Alex snorted. "Evidence? It's not a crime scene."

"Well, I doubt they're inviting people to stop by for photo ops," Katie said, her voice witheringly sarcastic. Lydia felt her insides tighten. Don't blow this for me, Katie, she wanted to tell her friend but Katie stared off into the distance, as though she'd already left the conversation.

"Whatever," Alex replied and Kyle let out a noise that was somewhere between a burp and a laugh.

"Gross!" Katie got up from the table.

"Where are you going?" Lydia felt half-dazed, as though just being in Alex's vicinity were a drug. The thought of pulling herself away from his warm side was chilling, and not just because the sun had dropped lower and the air was cooler.

"I don't know but are you coming?"

"Are you coming?" Kyle mimicked in a high-pitched voice. "Come on, Lydia, my little puppy." He snickered. Alex coughed, but it might have been hiding a laugh.

"Katie, you're so bossy you could be the mayor's daughter," Kyle continued. He frowned, then added, "Oh, wait. You are!"

"Whatever," Katie glared at Kyle and grabbed her drying towel from the nearby fence. "I'm out of here."

"Katie, wait," Lydia reached out to grab her friend's arm as she walked past. "I'll go with you."

Lydia didn't want to. Couldn't think of anything she'd less

rather do than walk home with Katie when she was in a bad mood. And having to leave Alex to do it made it a thousand times worse. But she'd been friends with Katie since, well, forever. And anyway, Kyle was being a jerk. As usual.

"Hold up, I'll walk with you guys," Alex said and stood up. Lydia felt like she'd been plunged into a snowbank, his warm skin pulled abruptly from her own.

"Thanks," Lydia said and smiled. At the same time, Katie yelled out, "Don't bother," and let the pool gate slam shut behind her, ignoring the small, neatly printed sign saying, "please shut gate gently."

"Katie!" Lydia called. "Ugh, sorry. I should—"

"No, it's fine. I get it," Alex said. "I'll grab my stuff. Meet you out front."

"Sure," Lydia said.

"Sure," Kyle mimicked then jumped over the table launching himself at Alex. He half fell, half righted himself, then grabbed Alex in a half-nelson. They laughed and wrestled, big feet flattening the grass.

Lydia ran to the changing room and pulled her dry clothes on, wishing she'd brought a sweatshirt and jeans instead of shorts and a T-shirt. At least she'd worn socks and her old combat boots instead of sandals. Her toes were bluish when she pulled her socks on.

Five minutes later, the trio was on the street. Katie was ahead, but not by much. This told Lydia everything she needed to know: Katie didn't want to be left out and was dragging her feet to get home, hoping Lydia would catch up.

"I'll be right back," she said to the guys then jogged ahead, catching up with Katie.

"I'm sorry John didn't show."

"Whatever. He probably realized finally what an ass Kyle is and made new friends."

"Um, doubtful," Lydia said. "Since they've been best friends since like, kindergarten."

"Whatever," Katie said again. "I can't stand him!"

"He has been extra dumb tonight," Lydia agreed. "But don't go home. Let's do something."

"Like what? It's too early for a movie, the general store's closed…there's nothing to do in this stupid, God-forsaken place."

"I know. But I don't have to be home till six. We still have like, an hour. Come on, Katie. Don't be boring."

Katie snorted. "You're the one who's boring. And since when did you and Alex get so friendly?"

Lydia's cheeks stained red and Katie finally relented.

"Sorry. I'm being a little witchy. I just…I can't stand Kyle. And John didn't even show up, so this whole afternoon is totally shot."

"Not necessarily. I'm here," Lydia swung an arm around her friend's shoulders. "Let's go down to the crash site. We can make it there and back by six and you can come over for dinner afterward. My mom loves it when you join us."

The truth was Lydia loved it even more. It turned the quiet, struggling-for-conversation meals into something that felt halfway natural.

Katie was quiet a second, then said, "Okay."

"Yay!" Lydia squeezed her friend's arm. "I owe you one."

Katie snorted. "One? I'd say a dozen for having to spend another hour with Kyle."

"Wait up, I'll tell the guys."

"Fine."

Katie stayed rooted where she was while Lydia walked back to where Kyle and Alex ambled along.

"Let's go to the crash site," Lydia said. She had no interest in seeing the car or whatever was left of Sheriff Rinko. But if it meant another hour with Alex, it was worth it.

"Cool," Kyle said. "Finally, Katie is cool about something for once."

"Shut up, Kyle," Katie called.

He gave her the finger.

Lydia looked at Alex. "Sound good?"

He nodded and then smirked. "Getting Kyle to shut up always sounds good to me."

They laughed. Kyle snorted and jogged ahead.

"Hey, Katie," he called out. "Wanna see what you're going to look like in eighty years? I got this new app and you're a total bag."

***

Lydia smelled the lake before she saw it. There was a distinct change in the air: from the pine and flowery smells of the woods to the smell of wet sand, hot stones with a slightly fishy undertone. They'd taken a shortcut from town, bypassing the thickest parts of the forest on a well-used trail that led to the narrow dirt road high above Gargun's Footstool. Lydia had always loved coming to the lake with Dad. It was the one thing they'd had in common—their curiosity of the gargun and a shared love of fishing—but she'd rarely come here since he'd left.

Well, maybe it was time to make new memories with new

people. Anyway, fishing with your father is something little kids did, not teenagers.

"I used to fish here with my dad," Alex said, as though he'd read her mind. "Me and my brother used to take turns driving the boat."

"That's cool," Lydia said, but in her chest, she felt a squeezing sensation. For one horrible second, she thought she was going to start crying.

"Woah, look," Kyle said. Lydia was grateful for the distraction. He pointed toward the bottom of the ravine. "It's still smoking."

Katie snorted. "Of course, it's still smoking. It only happened a few hours ago."

"Come on," Alex said and grabbed Lydia's hand. "Let's get down there."

"How?" Lydia asked, but Kyle was already running toward a small cluster of three boulders beside a rusted guardrail.

"There's a path down here," Alex replied and let go of Lydia's hand to climb over the stones. He reached his hand back up to help her and Katie down.

"I'm good," Katie said ignoring his hand. But then her foot slid over a smooth part of the boulder and she grabbed his hand, let him help her over it.

"Thanks," she said reluctantly and pulled her hand away as soon as she'd steadied herself. Lydia's hand felt lonely suddenly until Alex grabbed it again. His was warm and big, his palm slightly damp. But Lydia didn't mind.

They maneuvered their way down the ravine slowly. Katie's sandals slipped and slid over loose stones and bare rock and more than once Alex or Kyle or Lydia put out a hand to steady her.

"This is so stupid," Katie said for the fourteenth time. "We should go."

"What's the matter, Katherine, are you scared?" Kyle laughed. Then he lowered his voice to a stage whisper. "You know what they say about Gargun's Footstool, don't you?"

They were close to the hulking, smoking debris, now, the smell of burned fabric and metal and paint thick in the air.

"They say that the gargun lives in these rocks. That he comes out a night when there's a full moon and stalks along the cliff, grabbing anyone who walks by. Then he brings them back to his lair to torture them before he turns them into one of his demons."

Katie snorted. "Who'd be stupid enough to walk out here after dark? The ravine is a death wish. Anyway, he's supposed to be a water monster, idiot."

Alex laughed. "She has a point," he said.

The group reformed from a single file line around the outskirts of the crash site. The sheriff's car was barely recognizable. The paint was burned away, the metal frame of the car blackened. It had landed on its roof which had been pushed in so far that the door frames were half their regular size. The driver's side door—or what had been the door—was missing. It was hard to see anything in the dim interior, but Lydia imagined the shape of a body still inside the smoldering car.

"Do you think…do you think they were able to get his body out?" Katie asked.

"Yeah," Lydia exhaled. "See all the jagged parts around the door? They used the jaws of life to get him out." Her father had been a volunteer firefighter and Lydia had always been equal parts terrified of and fascinated by the jaws of life.

"But they still have to get a truck with a crane to get the car out. No other vehicle can get down here," Alex nodded toward the thick vegetation around them. "It's too hard to maneuver."

"Woah," said Kyle softly. "So, he like, died in there?" He nodded toward the crushed cruiser.

"Yeah."

"Sic."

"You're such a moron," Katie hissed in a whisper. For some reason, Lydia realized, they'd all been whispering.

"What do you think happened?" Lydia asked. She didn't feel good about being here suddenly. She'd known the sheriff, a little at least. He'd stop in and check on her and her mom from time to time, after Lydia's dad had left.

"Maybe he swerved to avoid a raccoon or something up there," Alex nodded to the road high above them.

"Or maybe he was drunk," Kyle offered.

Katie gave Kyle a scathing look. "Well, this is super exciting and everything but it's getting cold. Are you guys ready to go back?"

The boys both shook their heads and circled closer to the crash site. Someone—Deputy Pepper?—had cordoned off the area with bright orange tape. Must be the police department didn't have that yellow caution tape like they did in the crime shows. This orange stuff was what people used when they bought too-long boards at the hardware store and had to transport them home in their pickup trucks. They tied it to the ends so that the vehicle behind them wouldn't get lumber through their windshield if they drove too close and didn't see them.

Lydia's father had shown her how to tie it on so that it didn't come loose. They'd made a lot of runs to the hardware store for boards and nails and other things that the cabins were constantly in need of.

A shudder ran up Lydia's back as she followed the guys closer to the site. She didn't want to look, didn't want to see where Sheriff Rinko's body had been but at the same time she did. A rock skittered down from far above where they stood. Lydia glanced upward but didn't see anything. Maybe a squirrel was after a runaway acorn.

"...right there!" Kyle was saying and jabbed Alex in the side with his elbow. Alex shoved him back and Kyle nearly fell into the orange tape.

"Oh yeah, I see it now," Alex said as Lydia drew closer.

"Guys, come on!" Katie hissed, rooted in her spot. "This is stupid!"

Everyone ignored her.

"What do you see?" Lydia asked.

"Blood," Kyle and Alex answered in unison.

"Right there," Kyle said and pointed toward the hole where the driver's door had been.

Lydia squinted but couldn't see anything. There was too much dark, tangled metal, too much ash to make out what Kyle was pointing at. But she nodded her head anyway.

Kyle and Alex discussed the impact—would the sheriff's head have exploded like a watermelon or had the old cruiser had an airbag that would have smashed his face in?—and Lydia looked around them. The air was definitely colder down here and the smell of fish stronger. The sun had dropped further in the sky.

She had to go. She didn't have a watch on but was sure it must be getting close to six. And they still had to hike out and get back to town—Another rock fell from above them, this time closer.

Lydia glanced toward the sound.

Her breath stopped.

Something was there. A shape, a shadow pressed into the side of the mountain.

She grabbed at Alex's arm wordlessly, her fingers digging into his forearm.

"What?" he turned toward her.

She looked wildly from him back to the side of the cliff. She'd half expected the figure to be gone, but it wasn't. It stood—crouched really—peered down at them.

"There's someone there," she jabbed a finger toward the shadowy shape.

Alex squinted, cocked his head.

Kyle laughed. "What, like the gargun spying on us?"

"No, shut up man. I see it too. Right there." Alex pointed toward the shape and it moved, blended into the rocks around it until, when Lydia blinked and looked again, it was gone. As though it had been absorbed into the stone face of the ravine.

"It's probably just Dicky Jones," Kyle said with a laugh.

Lydia's legs shook and her heart fluttered hard in her chest. Home. That's where she wanted to be right now.

"Let's go," she said.

"Come on," Kyle said incredulously with another half-laugh. "We just got here!" He stooped over, picked up a few rocks, and threw them hard toward the spot. The first two clanked against stone, and the third disappeared into the undergrowth.

"Hey, Dicky!" Kyle yelled. "I've got more where that came from."

"I've gotta get home for dinner or my mom will kill me," Lydia said.

"So, go," Kyle said. He dusted his hands together and turned back to the wreck. "I want to get a little souvenir."

"You're such an imbecile, Kyle." Katie had come up behind

them without Lydia hearing her. She wanted to hug her friend.

"I have to go," Lydia repeated and hoped Alex would take the hint and offer to come back with them.

"Uh, sorry," he twisted his face into a look of half-apology. "I'm going to stay a little longer."

"Oh, okay," Lydia hoped her voice didn't give her away.

"Come on," Katie said, grabbing her arm. "We'll be fine."

"See you tomorrow?" Alex asked, one leg already over the tape barrier. "I'm working the same shift at the pool. Maybe you can stop by."

"Yeah maybe," Lydia said. Her heart had plunged to her toes. She didn't want to climb this cliff alone—or rather with Katie and her slippery, sliding shoes—and go anywhere near the area where whoever—or whatever—was hidden there.

As though reading her mind again, Kyle's eyes strayed upward toward where they'd seen the shadowy creature.

"Dicky Jones," he said again. "Even the town drunk wants to check out the action. He's probably here to spit on the sheriff's final resting place. Rinko locked him up so many times…"

Kyle's voice faded as he moved toward the car.

Lydia looked back up, but there was nothing there. Maybe it had been Dicky. Or a trick of the light. The way the sun had been hitting the stone. As much as she loved stories of the gargun, Lydia didn't believe in Kyle's stories about Gargun's Footstool, or that anything stalked the cliffs at night.

Still, she shivered as she grabbed Katie's arm and they started back up the trail. Maybe it would make sense to go through the thick undergrowth and end up by the beach, then take the driveway up to the road?

"Let's go the long way," she said, pointing toward the pine tree-laden woods that separated them from the beach beyond.

"It will be easier and we can get back on the main road quicker."

"Sure," Katie said. "Whatever will get us out of here fastest."

Chapter 9

Alex Richardson

"Come on, man," Alex said again. But Kyle ignored him, the same way he had the last two times Alex had told him to hurry up.

"I should have brought a hacksaw or something," Kyle complained. He'd been trying to twist a small, broken part of the car's fender off for what seemed like hours. Alex felt like leaving him there, but part of him didn't feel good about walking out of the ravine alone. Which was stupid. Nothing was up there. He looked again at the cliff, to the spot where Lydia had pointed. There wasn't anything there...was there? Something had moved just now but not in that same spot.

This was lower down.

Closer to the crash site.

Nearer to them.

Alex squinted but couldn't see anything. Dusk was another hour or so away, but clouds had moved in over the lake and the rocky cliff stood in shadow. Alex shifted from one foot to the other and tried to distract himself. Lydia was kind of cute. Not like Stella Sayers, but cute in her own way. She had a good body too. He'd had plenty of time to check her out from the lifeguard chair. And she was into him. He was sure about that. John had told him weeks ago that one of Katie's friends thought he was hot, but he hadn't been able to figure out which one. And John said Katie wouldn't tell him.

But John had had to fly to Vancouver for his grandmother's funeral which left Alex with only Kyle to hang out with. Kyle was more John's friend than Alex's but whatever. He was chill most of the time. Except when he completely ignored you.

"I'm heading out, man," Alex backed up a few steps. "I gotta get home and take a shower. I feel like the pool."

"Just a sec," Kyle said. "I've almost got—"

There was a faint metallic click.

"Ha! Got it!" He held something small and dark over his head in victory. Alex assumed it was the piece of the fender.

"Great, let's go."

"Don't you want one?"

"No," Alex's voice sounded more like his father's than he liked.

"What's the matter? Scared to be out here after dark?" Kyle grinned. His face was smudged with soot and his clothes were covered in it as he walked back toward Alex. He held up a small, triangular piece of blackened metal.

"Got it," he said again. "Wait till I show John."

"Yeah, he'll be stoked," Alex said.

"He will," Kyle nodded, the sarcasm lost on him. "I bet you no one else in town will have any—"

A sound cut through the evening air—part scream, part growl. All the hair on Alex's neck stood to attention.

"What was that?" Kyle's voice higher now, the bravado leaking away.

"I don't know. Maybe a wolverine."

"Nah, we don't have those here. A pine marten?"

74

"What's that?"

"You know…kinda like a weasel."

"Sure," Alex said, though he had no idea.

"Or it could have been a fisher cat," Kyle continued. "Those things sound—"

The noise sliced through the air again, closer this time.

"We should go," Alex repeated.

"Yup, let's."

They took a few loping steps in the opposite direction of the sound and jumped over the orange tape without bothering to pull it down. Kyle, who'd been a few steps behind Alex, sprinted toward the path where they'd come down.

"Nah man, we should take the road," Alex pointed toward the overgrown path where the girls had gone earlier.

"This way's faster, bro," Kyle said, moving toward the cliff.

But that's where the shadowy figure had been, Alex wanted to say but didn't. Instead, he followed Kyle. There was no way he was hiking out of here alone. Pine marten, fisher cat—who cared what it was? The sound was horrible, and Alex still had goosebumps on his arms and legs.

A little ball of sweat ran down between his shoulder blades, and he shrugged until it got soaked up by his shirt. What was his mother always telling him? "You see what you want to see." Sure, she usually mentioned it when he forgot to take out the trash…again. But it was true. He'd seen something up on the cliff because of all the stories he'd grown up with. Stories about the gargun living down here, waiting to grab passersby. And because they'd been talking about it earlier, that was all.

To the left of the boys, the trees started to shiver. Alex couldn't feel any wind when their leaves crashed together. Alex stopped in his tracks and stared.

A figure stood half-hidden in the undergrowth near the trees. It was slightly bent, like an old person with a permanent curve in their spine. But big. Way too big to be a little old person. It was dressed in black or dark gray—it was hard to make it out in the shadows—some sort of robe. Just as Alex was about to grab Kyle's arm his friend yelled.

"What the—"

"Run!" Alex shouted.

Rocks skittered under their sneakers as they turned abruptly to the left, zigzagging across the face of the rocky ravine. Scraggly bushes, anemic trees, and clumps of persistent tall grasses sprouted here and there among the rocks. Alex couldn't hear anything except their breath loud in his ears and the swish and snap of branches as they plowed over them and through them. Some scraped his arms and face, others grabbed at his ankles. Now it was Alex's turn to sprint, and he quickly passed Kyle, his time in the pool having strengthened his lungs and body.

"Hey…wait…" Kyle yelled. But pure fear fueled Alex. He couldn't have stopped if he'd wanted to.

And he didn't want to.

Alex panted, his eyes and cheeks burned from the leaves and twigs that slapped his face. They were beyond the steepest part of the craggy slope now and here the foliage and trees became thicker. He glanced behind him. Kyle's head was barely visible a few yards back. They'd run far from where they'd seen the thing but not far enough. Alex pumped his arms harder. It felt like any second talon-hands were going to reach out of the overgrowth and snatch him or snag his ankles as he passed by hidden overhangs in the slag stone.

The sound came again, this time louder. A guttural scream.

It was so loud Alex wanted to clamp his hands over his ears.

It was close.

Much closer than before.

Alex didn't have air to yell. All his oxygen was going toward getting the hell out of the ravine. He had to start going upward. There was no way they'd be able to lose that thing in the woods—he needed to get to the road.

He wanted to laugh suddenly—he felt like Ichabod Crane, running from the headless horseman. If he could just get over the bridge—

Kyle cried out suddenly. Alex paused, midstride, and nearly fell. He looked back wildly but couldn't see anything through the tangled bushes and snarled tree branches. He should stop, should retrace his steps. Kyle might have fallen. Or been caught.

But adrenaline spurred Alex on.

He was so close to the road now. His legs burned and he could feel wet tracks of something—blood?—running down the front of his shins. A branch snapped back and hit him in the face and the whole world turned green for a few seconds until he batted it away. The rusted guardrails were just ahead and to his right. A few more yards...

Kyle screamed.

The road was so close.

No, Alex had to go back. Had to—

The thing screeched again. Alex stumbled, nearly fell, righted himself.

He looked back again. A clump of bushes about five yards from where he stood shivered and shook. There was another sound, a horrible gurgling noise.

Kyle's scream ended.

It was very quiet.

Alex plowed upward, covering the last few yards with shaking legs. His sneakers scrabbled onto the road, and he paused for a second, winded. He glanced back over the side of the ravine. He couldn't see anything. And he wasn't waiting to.

Alex ran.

Chapter 10

Jessica Brown

...tales around the gargun date back to the earliest days of Stillwater's history. But is the creature monster or myth? Many old stories depict the gargun as a killer. As far back as the town's foundation, deaths and dismemberments are woven into local lore, steeped in local legend.

But many say the gargun is simply folklore, crafted by superstitious townspeople or those with overactive imaginations. Like many traditional fairytales, it could have been used to keep children from wandering the woods or down by the lake unattended. Perhaps, as the early witch hunts proved in a more famous New England town, the fear of something is greater than the actual presence of something.

Tarnishing its credibility further is the supposed form that this creature takes. Some say that the gargun appears as a large fish, growing legs and coming ashore to feed on animal and sometimes human prey under certain moons. Others insist that the creature resembles a sinister merman, remaining in the deepest parts of Stillwater Lake and snatching swimmers who attempt to cross the lake's width, dragging them down to a watery grave. Still, others report a dark-cloaked figure that huddles on the cliffs high above the lake, waiting for unsuspecting victims...

Jessica shivered and paused with her finger mid-page turn. Where did people come up with these things? She was half-tempted to toss the book aside. But that would mean she'd focus on one of two things: either the terrible crash she'd seen earlier today or the laptop sitting on the kitchen table.

She'd needed something to clear her mind from the day. That's what she'd told herself when she'd sat down with *Monsters of New England: Mystery or Mis-Information?* the large hardback book she'd balanced on her lap for the past twenty minutes. She'd intended to read just a few pages and then get to work on the outline for her own book. The laptop's fan stopped whirring and the screen went dark as she stared at it. Even it had given up on her and her procrastination.

"You'll be fine," Theresa had insisted over the phone on the last call Jessica had had with her agent before leaving. "You're a professional. You always get your mojo back. This trip is just what you need."

Now, Jessica took a sip of her tea and grimaced. Brandy wasn't her favorite spirit, but she'd found a half-full jar of it shoved far back in the cupboard and added a little to her tea. Just today, she reasoned. It had been a bad one after all. Images of the accident scene and the billowing smoke filled her mind. She took another sip, the hot liquid coating her stomach and loosening her limbs. She and Vic had reported the accident and then he'd driven her to the café on Main Street. They'd talked about his work mostly, tried to distract themselves from the awfulness of what they'd seen. He'd told her about the documentary he and his crew were going to film in the area, where he was from. He was a real chatterbox in fact, and Jessica, who usually found the trait tedious, had been happy for the distraction.

"They'll be arriving tomorrow," he'd said of his crew which sounded pathetically small to her.

"I'd be happy to introduce you. Actually, if you'd like to be part of the production, we're looking for a few interviewees. Mostly locals of course, but I'm sure we can make an exception." He'd smiled at her with his ultra-white teeth. Jessica had felt her heart sink. The last thing in the world she wanted to do was appear on camera and announce to the world where she was.

Being a best-selling author wasn't the same as being a true celebrity. She wasn't often hounded by the paparazzi or stalked by fans. But she was youngish, tall, and blonde. Plus, she'd been wildly successful with her last series, and the fact that she'd garnered a deal that was upwards of seven figures on the next-to-last book in the series was alone enough to make her clickbait. And after her very public, personal romantic tragedy...

"Thanks, but I think I'll pass," she'd told Vic. His eyes had widened slightly, and his smile had slipped. Certainly not the response he was used to getting, she'd thought. Didn't everyone want to be on TV and be famous after all?

Jessica sighed and picked the book back up. She'd found it at the general store that also served as a hardware/grocery/gift shop as well as a soda fountain.

"You can enjoy a root beer float and your favorite book while picking up bug spray and breakfast," the proprietress, a woman with shockingly bright red hair told Jessica. Indeed, the store was crammed with anything a visitor might need: from chemical spray for pesky wasps to a few aisles of canned and

81

boxed goods along with tiny tins of screws, nails, and hammers in several sizes. These were propped alongside tiny travel kits for sewing, glasses repair, even shoe polishing. Behind that, was a mini bookstore, packed chaotically full of books that ranged from summer beach reads to *A Tale of Two Cities*. When she'd seen the three titles of her own, Jessica had quickly exited the book area, with a monster book still in her hands.

She took another sip of tea and resumed the story she was reading.

...but what is fact and what is fiction? Accounts of the gargun range so greatly in detail and description that it is hard to pinpoint the truth from fantasy. Does the gargun sport fins and lurk in the lake's deepest depths? Or does he walk upright on two feet, a cross between man and spirit, waiting to claim its victims unaware—

A knock sounded on the door, three rapid ones in quick succession.

Jessica jerked, nearly dropping the book. She crossed to the window and peered out. Through the sliver of curtain, she could see a woman with brown curly hair that was slightly graying. She wore a white dress shirt and black pants, like a waitress. Something about her looked familiar to Jessica.

"Hello?" the woman called softly and knocked again. Her shirt was coming untucked in the back and was a little wrinkled. It looked too hot to wear in the middle of summer, even in the cooler evening air.

Jessica hurried to the door and opened it. "Hello," she said. "Sorry, I was just...putting something away."

"Hello, Ms. Brown. I'm sorry to disturb you. I'm Penelope Donovan, the owner of Cedar Grove Properties. I just wanted to check in and make sure you were settling in okay. See if there was anything you needed?"

"That's kind of you. Please, come in, Penelope," Jessica stepped back from the door.

"Penny, please, and that's all right. I don't want to disturb—"

"You aren't disturbing me at all," Jessica motioned to the kitchen where most of the boxes had been emptied and put out of sight. "I'm having tea, would you like some?"

"No, I…" The woman's dark eyes were ringed with darker shadows and her lips had a dry, pinched look. "Well, maybe just a small mug. If it's no bother."

"It's no bother at all. I was just reading and could use a break. I sit too much."

Penny laughed. "I don't sit enough." She twisted her wedding band around her finger twice, then glanced down and dropped her hands to her sides.

"It's been a crazy day…well, crazy week. Maybe make that month."

Jessica smiled again and motioned Penny to the table, setting her teacup on the opposite side. "Please have a seat."

Penny settled herself on the edge of the chair, looking like she might leap up at any moment. Jessica went to the stove and replaced the teakettle on the burner, found a mug, and dropped a new teabag in it.

"Are you all rented out?" Jessica asked.

"Yes. We had one unexpected cancellation, but I just got it filled. That's why I'm so late in getting up here. I like to be the one greeting all our guests when they arrive, showing them the lay of the land. But things were so hectic at the office—anyway," she sucked in a breath. "I'm sorry, I'm rambling. I hope Doogle—I mean, Lydia—was able to answer any questions that you had?"

"She did. She's very charming."

"Thank you. She's a little too smart for her own good sometimes."

"Aren't all teenagers?"

Another faint smile from Penny. "Do you have any?"

"No. No children."

"Of course, I'm sorry. You look much too young for teens anyway."

"Hardly. But I've never…well. No kids for me."

Penny cleared her throat. Her cheeks had turned pink. "How's the cabin? I hope it's what you expected?"

"Oh yes. Even better. Really, the photos don't do it justice."

"Good. That's good to hear. I always like to under-promise and over-deliver."

Jessica plucked the kettle off the stove as it started to shriek and set the mug of tea in front of her guest.

"Milk or sugar?"

"Oh, no thank you."

"I'll be right back," Jessica retreated to the living room for the book.

She set it on the kitchen table. "I picked this up at the general store," she said, turning the book so Penny could read the title.

"Oh dear," Penny said and then laughed. This time it sounded real though, not the brittle, polite attempt she'd made earlier. "I hope Lydia didn't scare you too much with that nonsense."

"No, not at all. It's…fascinating."

"That's a good word. My husband, well, ex-husband, was just that. Fascinated with folklore. He filled Lydia's mind with the old stories, embellishing them as time went on until now, she talks about it like it's fact, not fiction."

"You don't believe in it?"

Penny shook her head and took a small sip of tea. "Not a bit. But the festival is great for business."

Jessica nodded. "I'm not much of a believer, I figure there's enough scary stuff in the world without making up more. I bought this on a lark, more to pass the time than anything else." *And to avoid working on your manuscript*, a nagging little voice in her head chimed in.

It was quiet for a few seconds as each of them sipped their tea.

"Did you happen to hear the news about the accident?" Penny asked.

"I—yes," Jessica said. She wasn't sure why but didn't want to talk about her first-hand experience of the crash site and the still-blazing car.

"Do they know what happened?" she asked.

"Just a misjudgment on the road above, we assume. It was the sheriff—I'm not sure if you knew that—and his wife is just devastated. Poor Marie. They'd been together for ages. It's so hard to lose someone you love like that, unexpectedly too—"

Penny twisted her wedding band again, but then stopped and again dropped her hand. "Anyway, I just wanted to reassure you that everything was okay, well, I mean not dangerous or anything like that. One of the few bad things about living in a small town is the rumor mill. In case you've heard something else, I wanted to clear things up. There was no foul play suspected or anything like that."

Jessica nodded. Lady, murder is the norm in New York City, she thought but didn't say aloud.

"I appreciate the tea, but I really should be going. Lydia is old enough to stay by herself, but I get nervous leaving her alone at night still. Mother hen and all that."

"That's nice," Jessica rose too. "I wish more mothers felt that way. My agent likes nothing better than leaving her kids with the nanny every chance she gets."

Immediately, Jessica kicked herself mentally. She hadn't meant to let that slip and hoped Penny wouldn't notice.

"A nanny," Penny had a tinge of awe in her voice. "I can't imagine."

Jessica led Penny to the door and opened it, the knob cool beneath her palm. She debated with herself about the other thing that she'd heard, the sounds outside the cabin. Should she tell Penny? Maybe the other woman had some reasonable explanation that Jessica hadn't thought of. On the other hand, she didn't want to look like a pathetically helpless city slicker.

"You know, I thought I heard something last night," Jessica tried to make her voice casual. "Maybe it was just the fact that I'm on my own here in the sticks."

Penny's face fell.

Jessica laughed weakly. "Sorry. I only meant it's different here than the city."

"It takes more than that to insult me," Penny smiled but a crease formed between her eyebrows. "I love it here but know that it's not for everyone. I'm not sure what you could have heard. We don't often have bears here, but it could happen. Be sure to make noise when you're out, even just a whistle or hand clap now and then, just in case. They aren't vicious or anything, but better safe than sorry. They're more frightened of us than we are of them."

Jessica nodded but doubted that very much.

"If you hear anything else or if you need anything at all, please stop by the office or give me a call. Lydia told you about the cell signal?"

Jessica nodded again. She did feel like a silly city slicker, but also relieved. A bear was preferable to the gargun. "She did, yes, and thanks again for checking in on me."

"My pleasure," Penny said. "Enjoy the cabin. I'm sure I'll see you in town sometime soon. Will you be coming for the festival?"

Of course, she will! Anything to avoid writing, the little voice in Jessica's brain cackled.

"It will still go on?" Jessica asked. "I mean, after the accident?"

Penny nodded. "As far as I know."

"Well, then yes. I'm planning on it."

"Great. Sunday is the parade but the biggest event is probably Friday. That's when we have the opening ceremonies and the fireworks down by the lake. It's really very beautiful."

"Maybe I'll see you and Lydia there."

After Penny had left, Jessica locked the door and once again pushed the table close to it. She emptied her teacup and washed both hers and Penny's, then turned out the lights downstairs and climbed up to the loft. In addition to the large bedroom, tucked into the corner was a small bathroom with a clawfoot tub. The bathroom, like the rest of the cabin, had honey golden pine board walls. She avoided looking at the window where the bird had hit it and blocked out the image of the other birds lying dead on the lawn. She wondered if she should have told Penny about it, but the woman seemed to have enough on her plate already.

Jessica ran the water and undressed, slipping beneath the cloud of bubbles into the warm water. The brandy had loosened her limbs and the water washed away tension she didn't realize had stiffened her shoulders and upper back.

As she closed her eyes though, she saw the burning wreckage of the crash. Had it simply been an accident like Penny said? Jessica shivered despite the heat of the bathwater. The waitress at the little café in town had told Jessica and Vic that the location of the crash site was called Gargun's Footstool. And she'd told them the legend: how the gargun stalked the cliff there and snagged unsuspecting people on certain nights when the moon was full.

Jessica shivered, her bare skin above the water sprouting goosebumps as she remembered something else: last night, when the wind had rattled the windowpanes, a full moon had poked out from behind the thick sludgy-looking clouds.

She pushed the thoughts from her mind and tried in vain to dream up the opening to her book.

Chapter 11

Lydia Donovan

L ydia felt hot and cold at the same time. Was this even real? Had what Katie said happened, actually happened? She stared at the phone receiver in her hand as though it was a foreign object. Kyle was dead, Katie had told her, voice shaking. Right now, Alex was with his parents at the small station, being questioned about it.

Lydia shook her head. This couldn't be happening. They were just with those guys. How could Kyle be…be dead?

She stood up, walked around the living room. Her legs and arms felt numb, her brain felt thick and stupid. She looked down at her hands, wiggled her fingers to make sure they still worked. In the kitchen, she heard her mother humming as she did the dishes. They took turns every other night. Lydia walked through the swinging door separating the kitchen from the living room.

"Mom?" Her voice was too high and tight like it was right before she started crying.

Her mother turned from the sink, a cloud of soap bubbles dripping from her fingers. She had a rare smile on her face.

"Mom, Kyle…he's dead." Lydia shuddered and put her hands

to her face. Hot tears had started flowing and immediately her nose started running.

"What?" Her mother rushed to her, wrapping Lydia in her strong arms. "Oh honey, I'm so sorry. Was there an accident?"

Lydia couldn't answer, just nodded against her mother's shoulders.

"All right. Come sit down." Her mother wiped her dripping hands on a tea towel, then propelled Lydia onto the couch in the other room. Her arms were strong and Lydia felt the heat of her mother's skin through the wrinkled cotton button-down shirt. She closed her eyes, but the tears wouldn't stop coming. Her mother stroked her hair and murmured things Lydia couldn't hear over the sobs that wracked her body. She hadn't realized she was upset enough to cry but now she couldn't stop.

A few minutes later, after the jerking, spastic breaths had stopped, Lydia felt her mother's hand on her knee.

"I'm going to get you something hot to drink." She pushed a mound of fresh tissues into Lydia's hand. Lydia held them to her face all in a clump. They smelled like dust and dry grass.

"Here, drink this," her mother said and pushed a steaming mug into Lydia's hand minutes later. The sweet scent of chocolate rose from it, and Lydia, who'd finally stopped crying, wrapped her hands around the mug. They felt cold and clammy, like a dead body. She shivered.

"Can you tell me what happened?"

Lydia nodded. She felt weak now, wrung out, but also calmer. The question was: did she tell her mother that she'd been down at Gargun's Footstool poking around the accident site? Her mother would go ballistic.

"Kyle and a friend were down at the lake." Not a lie. "I think he must have fallen."

90

"He drowned?" Her mother put a hand over her mouth. "Oh, poor Margaret. I mean, not that a different way would make it better, but—"

"No, he fell while they were climbing, I think."

"Up the cliff at Gargun's Footstool?"

Lydia nodded. "I think so," she repeated, her voice barely audible.

Her mom made a frustrated sound in her throat.

"When are kids going to realize how dangerous that area is? Doogle, I better not ever catch you messing around on that cliff. The town really needs to do something about that area." She paused, then glanced from the window back to Lydia.

"Wait a minute. Was this connected to the accident this afternoon? Were those boys down there at the crash site?"

Lydia's mouth had turned dusty. She sipped the cocoa and shrugged her shoulders noncommittally. Sometimes she wondered if her mother had ESP or something.

"Well, it's a shame no matter what happened. Poor, poor Margaret and Jacob," she said again. "They must be devastated."

***

The line was ringing, and Lydia half hoped Alex wouldn't answer. It was nearly ten o'clock, far too late to be calling. Her mother would be mad if she found out. Lydia's heart pounded. She was tempted to hang up but wanted to hear Alex's voice, know that he was okay. One more ring, then she'd hang up. *Please, pick up. Please don't pick up. Don't pick up.*

"Hello?" Alex's voice.

"Oh, uh, hi, Alex. It's me. Lydia."

"Oh, hey."

"Hey."

There was a moment of uncomfortable silence.

"I was just calling to say that I'm sorry...about Kyle. I heard a little while ago. Katie told me."

"Yeah. Thanks." He sighed and Lydia imagined him running a hand wearily over his face.

"I'm, uh...I hope you don't mind me calling this late. I just wanted to...to make sure you were okay and everything. I mean, not that you're *okay*, okay, but—"

"Yeah, no thanks. That's cool of you. I'm fine. Well, I'm not fine like you said, but, yeah, I'm fine. They're still looking into it but so far it looks like I'm off the hook. I mean, I didn't do anything, you know? But they have to look at everything, I guess. And I mean, I was the only one down there, so..."

"Right," Lydia said. Her knowledge of the criminal justice system included scant amounts of time spent watching crime TV shows with her mother who loved them. Or used to, back when she'd watch TV in the evening. Now she only ever fell asleep in front of it.

"Did you, uh, see it happen?" Lydia asked.

There was another moment of silence.

"Hold on a second," Alex said. There was a quiet rustle, then the sound of muted voices, and then another rustle. A few seconds more, then Alex's voice came back on the line.

"Sorry. My little brother's being a pain. No, I didn't see it happen." Alex cleared his throat. When he spoke again, his voice was little more than a whisper. "But it wasn't an accident."

"What?" Lydia heard the disbelief in her voice and tried to cover it up. "What do you mean?" she said, lowering it an octave.

He was silent for a long minute. Then, "Remember that figure we saw—the shadow on the cliff?"

"Um, yeah." A tremor passed through Lydia's body. "Dicky Jones."

"Yeah, well, it wasn't Dicky. It was—I don't know what. The gargun, I guess. Whatever—that thing got Kyle."

There was silence again, so thick that all Lydia could hear was her heartbeat pounding away in her ears.

"Are you serious?" she asked finally.

"Yeah. It sounds crazy—I didn't tell Deputy Pepper—I just said that we'd seen someone up on the cliff earlier, or thought we had. He seemed pretty interested in that, especially when I told him the rest."

"What rest?"

"That the guy was following us. Stalking us, pretty much. I told him that Kyle hadn't just fallen but the dude had come after us and attacked Kyle."

"Did he?"

"Well, yeah. I guess. I didn't see it happen but I'm positive he killed him. We were almost to the road. We were running—" Alex's voice broke and then he cleared his throat and started again. "We were so close. But Kyle had fallen a little behind me. And I heard that thing—whatever it was—it screamed and then I saw the bushes moving…shaking you know? Like someone was being attacked. And then Kyle—"

Alex's voice stopped abruptly.

"He died?" Lydia asked.

"Yeah. Yeah, he didn't make it back out of there. I ran back to help him, but I couldn't find him. It's so thick in there, you know? Anyway, after that, I sprinted back to town. I've never run so fast in my life. It was…it was awful. Hearing him and…" Again, his voice fell away.

Lydia's hand was clenched so tightly over the receiver she

could feel the line from where the two pieces of plastic come together separating a little. She loosened her grip.

"What are you going to do now?"

"I don't know. Keep a low profile, I guess. My parents told me that the police might have more questions. We're not supposed to leave town or whatever. I don't know. It's crazy."

"Yeah."

"Deputy Pepper said that's just standard procedure when you've witnessed an accident."

"Do you think…" Now it was Lydia's voice that drifted away. Should she ask? If there was anyone who'd understand though, it had to be Alex.

"Do you think we really saw the gargun up there?"

"I don't know. But whatever it was, it was weird. And the sound it made when it was chasing me and Kyle? It didn't sound human."

Lydia shivered. She could picture Alex and Kyle scrabbling over the rock face of the cliff, a faceless, dark creature running after them. It could have been her and Katie. Or it could have killed Alex, too. Goosebumps in swatches broke out over her legs.

Another thought struck her. "I wonder if they'll cancel the festival."

"I don't know. Maybe? But with all these tourists here…I don't know," Alex said again. "You should ask Katie."

"Right." It would be horrible to have the festival after two people had just died. On the other hand, Alex was right. There were a lot of visitors here from out-of-town. And the town needed the money that the tourists brought in, especially the festivalgoers who were known to buy just about every tchotchke, book, T-shirt, and gargun-named food item that shops in the area offered. What would it do to Mom's business if the festival was canceled? Still, how could the town go on and pretend like nothing happened?

"Lydia?" her mother's voice called from downstairs. "Are you still reading?"

Lydia put a hand over the receiver and called down, "No, I'm going to sleep now."

"Gotta go," she told Alex.

"Sure. Thanks for calling to check on me."

She smiled. "You're welcome."

After they'd hung up, Lydia lay in bed staring up at the ceiling. She was never going to fall asleep tonight. That was the last thought she had before she rolled over onto her side and closed her eyes.

But she did sleep and her dreams were filled with dark, shadowy creatures and fires and Kyle—annoying, laughing, screaming Kyle—falling over a cliff again and again.

Chapter 12

Vic Mellin

"Look, I get what you're saying about the shot. But I'm telling you it's not going to work," Nikki said.

Vic sighed and ran a hand through his hair. "But if we got the camera up higher, put a little angle on—"

"Not happening." Nikki's voice was firm, and her mouth was a flat line. She was usually easy to get along with despite the way she pushed herself. She was a born director and a competitive marathoner. Occasionally though, as was the case now, she would draw a line in the sand. And even though Vic knew it was futile, he'd been trying to persuade her to see his point of view for the past twenty minutes.

They were standing on the pebbled beach at Stillwater Lake. It was drizzly and the clouds overhead were thickening. Great, Vic thought. That's just what they needed. A downpour to finish off the crappy day. He'd been leading the small crew around the area for the past three hours, showing them the potential locations for filming. So far, Nikki hadn't been very impressed. Joe, her kid brother, hadn't said anything. That wasn't unusual. Nikki said enough for both of them.

Vic couldn't blame him. Usually, Nikki's instincts were dead on. It's just that Vic wanted so badly for the shots he'd picked to work. As producer and CEO, the bottom line was nearly as important as the film itself. He couldn't continue to make documentaries and get new gigs if the company went bankrupt. Vic ran a hand over his chin and scrubbed it a few times. He cursed Guy in his mind again.

This was too much. He couldn't be expected to be the face of Backyard Films and the CEO and the producer. The truth was he didn't know how much longer he could keep going like he had been. The late nights and early mornings, the travel and constant pressure of finding that "next thing" that was going to give the company a name. It had turned into a runaway train. Vic drank too much too often. He'd gained twenty pounds in the last year, his time at the gym giving way more and more to another few hours of work. When did it end?

"There," Nikki pointed toward a section of the lake covered in lily pads. "That's where we're likely to get some clean underwater footage."

Vic raised his eyebrows.

"Trust me," Nikki said. "Joe and I will take a couple of kayaks out and do some tests. It's more likely the water under those plants will be clearer, if for no other reason than it hasn't been as disturbed as the water out here." She nodded toward the dock. She had a point. Trucks and SUVs lined most of the beach with empty boat trailers shining in the sun.

"All right," he said. "But what about the still shots up on the mountain?"

"Yeah, one of those spots might work." Nikki glanced at her watch and sucked in a breath. "Here's Joe with the kayaks now," she looked toward the empty road, and soon Vic saw the van bouncing along, two bright orange kayaks strapped to the roof.

"Let's get this stuff cleaned up and then we'll—"

"No, go ahead and check out the lake. I've got this," Vic said.

"You sure?" Nikki raised her perfectly sculpted eyebrows and he nodded.

"Yeah. I'm going back into town afterward. Got a phone call to make. Meet you guys back there for some lunch?"

"Sure, sounds good."

"What time should I pick you up?"

"That's okay. We'll walk. I need to stretch my legs. Sitting isn't good for you." She looked at him out of the corner of her eye eying the gut overflowing his pants.

Nikki moved off to help her brother unload the kayaks while Vic re-packed all the equipment they'd used to do underwater test shots. Joe preferred to use a smaller camera with a simple setup to do his testing.

"What about the kayaks?" Vic asked.

"We'll leave them here after. The place we rented from said that they've got other people using them later today. We're supposed to chain them to that big tree when we're done." She pointed to a thick-trunked tree, that was missing half of its limbs. A thick, rusted chain was snaked around its base.

Vic put everything back into cases and loaded them into the van. It was old and had developed a rattle on the way here. Another expense. Vic sighed and slid the door closed.

He needed to clear his head. Get back to town and call the bank. Backyard Films had a line of credit that was just about tapped out and Jim, his loan officer, could smell desperation miles away. Vic would have to put on his salesman's hat and schmooze his way into another chunk of change to get the next show finished.

***

Nikki paddled her kayak quickly and then poked around in the lily pads, clearing an area for the submergible camera to go in. Joe was a few minutes behind her, so she yanked at the lilies and waited for him. Thunder rolled a long way away and the clouds above skittered in faster like they were racing each other toward the lake.

Fantastic. A rainstorm would be just perfect. Nikki sighed and shook her head. She was starting to sound like Vic and she didn't like it. Honestly? She was getting tired of this gig. Tired of constantly trying to be the positive one, of looking for the potential in every situation. She had enough stress in her personal life without taking more home with her.

And Vic. While they'd worked well together when she'd first landed the job, lately he was becoming more and more desperate. She got it. Money was tight and stress was high for him too. He looked and acted little like the guy he had when she'd taken the job. Then, he'd been ninety percent salesperson, a fitness buff with clean boundaries between work and personal life. He'd talked about success and progress and how quickly they would garner awards for their work. He'd only needed to suggest seeing her name on the big screen very soon for Nikki to feel happy sweat break out on her palms.

She'd taken this job because it was supposed to lead to something. Something else, something better. She'd anticipated attending Cannes Film Festival within a year. Two at the most. Smaller, independent film festivals and awards before that. But there'd been no sign of any of that happening.

Nikki swept the paddle through the lilies. Something heavy caught the tip of it. She pulled back on the paddle, but it wouldn't budge. Great. She sighed again and used the stuck paddle to draw the kayak closer to the spot in the water. The water was dark here, much darker than she'd anticipated. The murky sky ahead didn't help of course. Not like she was going to get blue water when the clouds above were the color of pewter. Still…

She tugged on the paddle again. This time she'd have sworn she felt something tug back. A fish? A turtle? She searched her memory bank trying to think of largish animals that lived in lakes. Maybe there were big crawdads here? It could have caught the tip of the paddle on its claw.

Nikki leaned forward, closer to the edge of the kayak. The hard, orange plastic side bit into her ribs as she peered into the water. She pushed her legs against the other side so that the whole thing didn't fall over. She couldn't see anything. The water might as well have been an ink pot.

Slipping her hand down the length of the paddle, Nikki extended her hand into the water. The kayak wobbled. She pulled again on the paddle. It didn't budge. Nothing moved on the other end, either. Nothing—

And then she felt it again. Pull, pull. Just like she'd done. She re-balanced the boat by tipping her weight slightly in the other direction, then gave three jerks to the paddle.

Whatever was under the water gave it three jerks back.

Nikki gasped.

A crawdad didn't know how to count. So, what in the world was—

"What's up?" Joe asked, finally gliding in beside her.

"My paddle is stuck…on something. But I swear I just felt it pull back."

Joe looked from Nikki into the dark water.

"You wanna go in?"

"No," Nikki said too loudly. She lowered her voice. "No, I don't want to go in. And I don't think you should either."

But Joe wasn't listening. He'd already pulled off his T-shirt and used it to tie their two kayaks together.

"Joe, don't," Nikki said, but he only grinned and jumped. The splash he made when he hit the surface sent both kayaks bobbing and sprayed Nikki completely.

"Idiot," she said but couldn't help smiling as Joe popped back up from the lake, a lily pad covering his head and one eye.

"It's pretty damn dark down here," he said. "You bring the underwater flashlight?"

"Yeah. Just give me a minute."

As Nikki turned to get it out of the bag the pressure on the paddle released. It surprised her so much that she almost dropped it.

"Hang on," she told her brother, trying to juggle the paddle and not let the kayaks get pulled further into the lake. She took a couple of quick strokes while Joe treaded water, then groped around in the canvas bag to find both the underwater flashlight and camera. Since he was already down there, he might as well get some decent footage. It might save them a trip later—

There was a huge splash and Nikki looked up in time to see Joe disappearing below the surface.

What—

Startled, Nikki dropped the bag back into the kayak.

"Joe?" she called. "Quit messing around. I found the flashlight for you. And the camera. You might as well get some footage..." her voice drifted off. Where was he?

"Joe?"

Nothing.

Circles on the lake's surface from when he'd gone under touched and then rippled out into larger circles. The lawn of lily pads bobbed up and down.

Idiot. He was just waiting for her to panic, to launch herself into the lake fully clothed.

"Joe, knock it off. This isn't funny!"

Well, he'd better think again. She'd fallen for his tricks too many times in their—

Suddenly the water roiled. Joe shot up out of it like he'd been blasted by a canon. He gasped, yelled once, something Nikki couldn't make out, and fell back into the water.

"Joe!" Nikki screamed. She used her paddle to get closer, then leaned again over the side. She had to go down there. Had to help him. Whatever had gotten the paddle must have grabbed Joe. She snatched the flashlight and shone it into the black water.

"Joe, I'm coming." Nikki tried to move into a crouch in the kayak, but it tipped and swayed so badly that she sat back down. She should bring something with her. A weapon. Were there eels in this lake? Sturgeon? She'd heard of the huge fish. They were nasty with sharp, jagged teeth. The lily pads would offer great camouflage. Could one have been hiding in the water and grabbed her brother?

"I'm coming!" Nikki cried again and this time used his boat to try to balance her own, give her enough leverage to get her legs free of the kayak so that she wouldn't overturn everything when jumping in.

She didn't have a chance to finish the maneuver.

Bubbles—hundreds of them—rose from the spot where Joe had gone into the water. Seconds later she saw his bare back pressing up against the lily pads. It was pale and covered in red scratches. She looked for his cap of brown curls. But between his shoulders, where his neck should have been was empty space. A red cloud had formed in the water. Nikki couldn't breathe.

Something moved in the crimson water. Something dark and sinewy. A figure—or was it just a shadow?—gyrated beneath her kayak.

Nikki's mouth formed into a scream. But she was pulled into the water before it ever made it to her lips. As the dark, cold water covered her, the last thing she thought was, *this cannot be happening.* Then icy talon-like fingers wrapped themselves over her own and pulled her down, down, down.

Chapter 13

Tony Bradford

"We're closing in ten minutes. Found what you needed I hope?" The middle-aged librarian looked at Tony over the edge of her hot pink reading glasses. Rhinestones sparkled at the corners and fuchsia strips in her graying hair matched the glasses. Her blue nametag read, "Rita".

"Yes, sorry," he glanced at the big wall clock ticking behind the circulation desk. "I didn't realize how late it had gotten."

"No worries," she said and snapped her gum twice. The noise was like an explosion in the too-quiet room. "I wouldn't normally mind staying a little later, but my boyfriend's picking me up for dinner at the Pine Needle. Been there yet?"

Tony shook his head. His finger held the spot on the page of the old, yellowing book that he'd been immersed in.

"Snack bar just outside of town. They have the best clam strips you've ever tasted and creemees the size of your head."

Creemee? It took Tony a second to remember. What the rest of the country called soft-serve ice cream, Vermonters referred to as creemees.

"Oh, uh, sounds great."

"Yeah, we're going over on his bike. He'll be here right at closing so..." Rita's voice drifted off and she glanced at the books and papers spread around Tony on the table.

"Right. Sorry. I'll get this cleaned up in two minutes. I'm nearly done the page," he nodded to the book.

"Sure, that's fine," she said and went back to tidying something behind the desk with another snap of her gum.

Tony re-immersed himself in the text.

... the town itself had a hard start as so many early settlements in New England. The harsh weather and long winters, along with disease, flooding, and starvation, led to many early deaths.

The town of Stillwater was founded by the Briggs and Johnson families, both of Boston. In fact, the first settlement was built on what was then referred to as Victory Road. Though the naming of the road was perhaps optimistic. Rather than wealth and a life of ease as both families and the others that soon followed them had enjoyed in the city, life in the northern Vermont wilderness was exceptionally hard.

There was little else of interest. Tony frowned as he closed the book. Victory Lane...had he seen that street sign somewhere? He didn't think so. Besides, when the town was founded, Tony doubted it had street signs. Still, the name rang a bell.

Victory Lane, Victory Lane...

"Excuse me," he called to Rita.

She looked up from the desk, peering at him over the bright glasses.

"I was just wondering—is there a map here from the 1700 or 1800s of the area?"

She smirked. "Well, there's the big one behind you."

Tony turned around and saw a huge, faded map fastened under glass. In the bottom left corner, he saw the date, 1809.

"Thanks." He gave her a sheepish smile and made a show of gathering up books while simultaneously looking at the map. As soon as Rita had gone back to whatever she was doing, he left the books and walked closer to the map. It was well preserved. Small boxes indicated the meager number of buildings in Stillwater at that time. Thin roads wound through the little gathering of boxes.

Across from the little town if you could call it that, was the lake. That at least hadn't changed much. Using the lake as his point of origin, Tony traced the roads. There was one main road—the largest of the bunch—called fittingly, Main Street, and a few others that sprouted off it. There was a Pine Ledge Road, a Knobb Lane, and Pleasant Street. And then far to the left, way up on the side of an incline was a line so thin that Tony had missed it the first time. Victory Lane.

Tony gauged it from the center of the little town. Something shifted and squeezed in his belly. The road and its location were familiar. Victory Lane was still in existence, although it had been renamed Raven Hill Road. He'd seen that on his hike the other day. It was where Jessica Brown's little cabin pressed up against the side of the mountain.

"Excuse me," Tony said again, this time picking up materials in earnest while Rita looked at him with a bemused expression. "Do you know anything about Raven Hill Road?"

"Sure," she said. She stood up and walked through the little half-door. It swung back and forth in her wake. "And before you ask, yes, it's where the very first townsfolk lived."

"I—" Tony stopped. "It is?"

"Yeah."

He stacked the books up neatly. "So, the cabin that's there now, on Raven Hill Road—"

Rita shook her head. "No, that's not original. It was built maybe in the early 1900s? You'd have to ask Penny Donovan to be sure—she's the owner. She and her family—well, her daughter now—run Cedar Grove Properties. They have a bunch of rentals in the area."

Tony didn't bother telling her that he was renting from Penny. Instead, he moved to pick up the largest books, but she got to them first, hefted them over his protests, and walked them back to the metal cart behind the counter.

"And now, Tony, I must kick you out." Rita dumped the books unceremoniously onto the cart which squeaked under their weight and grabbed her purse—also a shade of hot pink—and pulled out a pair of sunglasses.

"Sure, thanks again for your help."

The sweet smell of freshly cut grass and hot pavement hit him full force as he left the library. The sun was welcome after the overly-airconditioned building. He breathed in deeply, leaned against a lamppost, and tried to figure out what this meant if anything. Could that fact be tied to what she'd seen outside the cabin? But how could he justify his research without sounding like a stalker? "Oh, gee, Jessica, I was just researching where you're staying and...But it might be important. And even better, a little voice in his head said, it would give you a great excuse to see her again.

Tony was still thinking about it when a stuttering Harley picked up Rita and roared off, down Main Street.

Tony walked in the direction the bike had gone. Signs of festival preparation were everywhere. A large banner hung between two tall lampposts in the center of town, proclaiming

"The 49ᵗʰ Gargun Festival!". On the right side of the road, a man was sweeping the sidewalks with a big push broom. Two shopkeepers peered into a storefront window and pointed, chattering. Big urns filled with bright-red geraniums stood by every iron lamppost and each urn sported a tiny American flag. The gargun, it seemed, was also patriotic.

Tony passed the general store. It was festooned with large tissue paper flowers in muted shades of pink, cream, and baby blue under its covered porch. A large, handwritten sign in neat cursive announced, "Gargun items here! Games! T-shirts! Books! Souvenirs!"

He kept walking, then paused outside of the little café where a teen was handing a mom with three little kids ice cream cones from a screened window at the side. A woman was just about to enter the café by the front door, her blonde hair held up in a chic twist, dark sunglasses and a floppy hat hiding most of her face. She glanced back as she entered, then paused with the door still half open.

"Tony?" She waved.

He ignored the little electrical tremor that ran up his sternum.

"Hi," Tony walked toward Jessica. "How are you?"

"Good. I was just going to pick up something for dinner." Her smile widened. "Why don't you join me? I'm going to bring it down to the lake. It's a beautiful night."

"Sure," Tony replied. A little too eagerly? the voice in his head questioned. He ignored it. "Sounds great."

***

"So, the founders of Stillwater lived where I'm staying now?" Jessica pushed her sunglasses further up on her nose. It was hot

108

and Tony hoped that the air at the lake would be cooler. They'd opted to drive but had left the windows of Jessica's car open fully to get a breeze.

"It looks that way. I know it's a long shot, but I wondered if it could tie in somehow with what you saw the other night."

She made a noncommittal noise. "How could it?"

Tony shook his head. Now that he'd said it out loud it sounded stupid. Really stupid. Also, he was distracted by her perfume. He should tell her, he knew, about Meredith. Shouldn't he? But then, Jessica might not be into him. That would be embarrassing if he told her, and she blew him off.

He shook his head. Get it together, man. "No, you're right. Probably not connected. But there were men named Jenson Briggs and Claude Johnson. I learned about them at the Historical Society meeting."

"Oh no, I'm sorry!" Jessica slapped her forehead before dropping her hand back to the steering wheel. "I completely forgot."

"That's okay." Tony ignored the little fissure that rose in his chest. She hadn't meant to stand him up. She'd forgotten, that was all.

"You know, it's weird. I'm not into the whole gargun thing. But I do get this feeling at the cabin. The first night something broke the window. I told you that, right?" She continued when Tony nodded. "When I went to look at it I saw something, that is, I *thought* I saw something..." she stopped again, chewing on her lip. Then she glanced at Tony and laughed.

"I'm sure it was nothing. Just nerves, you know? It's so quiet here and so...so remote," she said the word like it was foreign on her tongue.

"What'd you see?"

Jessica shrugged, flicked the handful of thin, gold bracelets down to her wrist. They tinkled together. It reminded Tony of her laugh.

"I thought I saw something in the little grove of pine trees out front. And there was this weird light. More like a glow—and it was coming from that area. But you know, it could have been a thousand things."

"Like?"

"What?" She glanced at him, startled.

"Like what? I can't think of many things glowing in the night."

"Well. It could have been fireflies. Or maybe there's some solar nightlight out there or a bug zapper. Do people still use those? Anyway, I never went to investigate. More likely it was my imagination. Though I did hear…well. I thought I heard footsteps that night. Outside on the gravel." She bit her lip.

Tony saw goosebumps rise on her long, bare arms.

"You did?"

She nodded, glanced at him, then back toward the road. "I don't know." She shrugged again. "City mouse in the country. And I had had a couple of glasses of wine before—"

The car jerked suddenly as Jessica slammed on the brakes. Another vehicle, a white van, was driving fast up the narrow road toward them, overextended onto their side of the road.

"Stupid jerk," Jessica muttered and eased her car further to the right. "This road is horrible. I can't believe they don't do something to fix it. It's where the sheriff—"

"Hey, sorry," a man called from the van as it drew parallel to them. "I'm sorry. Look, do you have a phone with you?"

"Yes, but I don't think I can get a signal," Jessica said putting her window down further.

The man cursed, ran a hand through his hair.

"Vic?" Jessica asked.

The man leaned forward in the seat and peered at them.

"Oh, Julie."

"Jessica."

He grimaced. "Right, Jessica, sorry. I was meeting my crew down there, but they seem to be missing."

"Missing?"

"Yeah. I went into town to make a few calls and my friends took kayaks out to do some underwater shots. Only when I got back, they weren't there."

"Could they have gone further out on the lake?" Jessica asked.

"Or maybe around that bend?" Tony offered. They all glanced toward the lake. The largest part was shaped like a bowl, huge and round. But part of it wrapped up and around out of sight of the shore, even from the raised elevation they were sitting at now.

Vic shook his head. "No, I checked. One of the kayaks was back on shore—just a little way out—and I grabbed it and paddled around but there's no sign of them. Just the kayak and," he shrugged, and ran a hand through his hair again. "Nothing else."

"Do you want us to look?" Jessica asked.

"Nah. Well, just keep an eye out for them I guess," Vic said, distractedly. "If you see them—Nikki or Joe—could you give them a lift back to town?"

"Sure. Of course," Jessica said.

"Thanks," Vic said. "I'll go back to my room and see if I can get them on my cell. Signal's a little better in town." He gave them a halfhearted wave. "Thanks again."

"You're welcome," Jessica said, but Vic had already roared off. Jessica steered closer to the middle of the road away from the ravine and swore under her breath.

"Sorry," she said, seeming to remember Tony was there. "I hope they're okay."

"They probably just decided to film somewhere else and got their wires crossed."

"Yeah, probably." Jessica slid her window back up.

The car was nice, Tony thought. Really nice. A late-model Mercedes with all the bells and whistles. Cool air flowed out of the vents even though they'd had the windows open. The seats were cushy, and he suspected heated in winter.

Looking down at the lake, Tony noticed how dark the clouds were. It had been sunny and overly warm in town, but here, the sky was smudged with darkness. The lake formed stiff little whitecaps.

"Maybe we should rethink our dinner destination."

Jessica glanced at him.

"Or should we look for the missing film crew and put dinner on hold?"

"We could look around a little, in case."

Jessica nodded. "Yeah, let's do that."

She focused on descending the slope carefully. The clouds swirled lower and looked even darker over the lake. As the car crept down the incline, Tony half expected the spot where the land and sky met to open its mouth like a giant, dark beast, and swallow them up.

Chapter 14

Alex Richards

"We can't do that, imbeciles. It's crazy," Katie's voice was high-pitched, and she sounded on the border of hysteria. Alex leaned away, looking from the two girls to the playground beyond them. Evening was falling and most of the kids had gone home for dinner. Two little boys remained with a frazzled-looking girl with blonde hair. Alex didn't recognize her. Maybe a nanny that one of the families from out-of-town had brought with them.

A snap nearby brought Alex's attention back to the group. Lydia broke a twig into tiny pieces, each one measured to the same length.

"I think we should do it," she said softly. Katie groaned and let her head fall on her outstretched arms on the picnic table.

"Of course, you think that," Katie sounded pissed. "Because it was Alex's idea."

Lydia started to say something but Alex broke in.

"Look, you don't have to come. Either of you," Alex said. "But I need to. I'll always wonder if I don't."

"But it's crazy," Katie said again, lifting her head enough to look at Alex. One heavily lined eye peered up at him.

"How are you planning to get into the morgue without anyone seeing you? And what are you even looking for?"

"The mark that Lydia told us about."

Alex thought about their earlier conversation. Lydia had reminded them of the report she'd written in history class the semester before. She'd researched something called the devil's marks that were a big part of the European witch hunts. They'd also influenced the Salem Witch Trials. It had been thought, Lydia had said, that the devil left his mark—a scratch caused by either his talon or tongue—on the witch, sealing a pact between them. If any of the people arrested—mostly women—had this mark, they'd be automatically slated for execution.

"The gargun's 'sign'?" Katie's voice was incredulous. "Come on. That's complete BS."

Lydia shrugged but her cheeks got pink.

He rubbed a hand over his cheek. "It's not just that. I want to see if there's any other evidence—you know, that he didn't fall. Or at least, he didn't just fall. All I need is for you to create a diversion. And then I'll go in and look. It will take five minutes, tops."

"I'll go with you," Lydia said. "If you want."

"Sure, yeah, whatever." He tried to keep his voice nonchalant but felt relieved. Even though the plan was his, it wasn't anything he looked forward to. Sneaking into the town's morgue would be hard enough to pull off. And then looking at Kyle's dead body—Alex shut his eyes momentarily. What would that be like?

Still, he had to know.

"How are you going to find anything?" Katie asked as though she'd read his mind. "I mean, Kyle—he's likely to be pretty messed up."

"I don't know, just anything like claw marks, puncture wounds—"

"Claws?" Katie snorted. "You think the gargun has claws?"

"I don't know, Katie, I didn't spend a lot of time inspecting its hands while it was chasing us." Alex's throat felt hot and tight. He could do this without them—without either of them—but it would be easier to do it with them.

"We should keep it simple." Lydia was no-nonsense. "Katie creates a diversion, then you and I slip in," she glanced at Alex, and he nodded. "We find his…his remains and have a quick look, then get back out fast. There's a rear entrance to the building. That would be the best way to get in and out. It's never locked."

"How do you know that?" Katie asked and pulled herself into a slouch. Alex sipped the mostly warm bottle of soda and wondered the same thing.

"My dad was on the volunteer fire crew, remember?"

"Oh yeah," Katie responded. "I forgot about that."

"They had to use the morgue occasionally. Once he brought me to see it."

"No offense, but your dad's weird." Katie rolled her eyes.

"So, we're doing it?" Alex asked.

Lydia nodded. A second later, Katie did too, her dark ponytail bobbing in the dim light.

"All right," Katie said. "But now, before I lose my nerve."

***

Though Katie had initially protested being the one to create a diversion, Alex was pretty sure she loved the idea. Always the lead in the school plays, Katie was like a drama queen on overload. Her and Lydia seemed about as different as they could be from each other. Alex was just glad it was Lydia going with him into the morgue and not Katie. She wasn't the type who'd be squealing and jumping around at every little sound like Katie was.

Lydia, it turned out, was pretty chill. When his hands had been too sweaty to open the big door, Lydia had stepped in. Alex had followed...and kept following. He'd heard the term, "out of body experience," before. But it wasn't until he was standing over the thick, black plastic shroud that he understood it. It was like he watched someone else unzip the bag, saw someone else clamp a hand over his mouth. Like he floated above his body. Lydia gasped quietly when they'd unzipped the body bag but she—unlike Alex—had quickly recovered.

An unwelcome feeling of dread and shame covered him as he stared into the bag his stomach tipping sideways. Was this his fault? Could he have saved his friend if he'd turned back instead of running away? No. He hadn't run away, he reminded himself. He'd just run.

"Poor, poor Kyle," Lydia murmured. They were quiet for a few long, cold seconds.

Then she said, "Let's hurry up and get this over with."

Alex had tried not to think about what Kyle would look like. Even without wanting to though he'd imagined his friend looking beat up: expected a few bruises, some scrapes, and cuts. But the body was in worse condition than that. Scratches and cuts did cover most of Kyle's torso. His face was badly bruised and dried blood had clumped in his hair and most of one side of his face. There was something wrong with his skull, in the area where the dried blood was. Most of his skin was purple with bruises.

Alex peered more closely and then stepped back and gagged.

"What?" Lydia asked. She'd moved to the other side, was looking at Kyle's hands and forearms.

"His...his head." Alex didn't even recognize his voice.

Lydia's eyes moved to where he'd pointed and grew wide. "Maybe that's what killed him."

The area of Kyle's head was sunken in, the skull caved in where it should have been rounded. What had done that? Had it happened while he was alive or afterward when his body had tumbled down the ravine? And had his body really fallen or had the thing...Alex shivered. Had the thing tossed him there after it killed him? Alex tried to stop the image of his friend falling, tried to block out the sound of his screams when the gargun had gotten him.

"Look," Lydia said. "What's that?"

Alex didn't want to look anymore. He thought he was going to puke. The room was too small and the walls were closing in. He couldn't breathe. Even if he did, he couldn't take another minute of the horrible smell. His fingers had turned light blue he noticed when Lydia grabbed his hand.

"What?" he managed to get out. He couldn't ralph in front of Lydia. He already looked like a total dork. But he needed to get out of this place. Now.

"Right there. See that mark?" Lydia pointed to a thick red curved mark above Kyle's collarbone. At first glance, it looked like a deep, red gash.

"So what?" Alex said.

"That's it. It looks exactly like what I wrote about in my report.

Alex looked again. "I don't know. Couldn't it just have been a branch or something?"

"Yeah, but look at this," she pointed to the mark again. Alex wanted nothing less than to look at it again but braced himself on the metal table beneath Kyle's body and looked where Lydia pointed.

"If that was made by a branch or stone or something, it would be jagged, right? I mean, if it was from Kyle falling, then whatever the thing was—wood, stone, whatever—it would have torn at his skin. Look how perfectly formed this is," she pointed again and traced the mark while her finger hovered over Kyle's skin.

"I don't know," Alex repeated.

"There's only one way to be sure," Lydia said. She pulled out an ancient-looking flip phone and took a couple of photos of the marks. Then she moved to another of the three drawers that lined one wall of the small room.

"What are you doing?" Alex whispered.

"I'm going to see if the sheriff has the same mark." Her voice was a whisper.

"What? That's not a good idea. We need to get out of here, Lydia, there's no time to—"

"I'll be quick," she said and before he could respond, she'd checked the tag on the other two doors and pulled the middle one open.

Cold sweat popped out on Alex's neck. The feeling of nausea had faded slightly but now, faced with the prospect of looking at another dead body, returned in full force.

"Close him up," Lydia said over her shoulder. "We need to leave as soon as I'm done."

Alex stood frozen, as Lydia, her hand shaking slightly, unzipped the second black bag.

"Oh, ugh," she said quietly and turned her face away. Then

she took a deep breath and peeled back the two sides of the bag, looking at the body inside. Alex couldn't see from his position what she was looking at, but hurriedly zipped up the bag protecting Kyle. With his own hands shaking, he shoved the long table holding his friend's body back into the drawer, and closed it softly.

"Look, he's got one too," Lydia's voice was too loud in the quiet space.

"Shh," Alex said automatically and willed his stomach to not dump its contents as he moved closer to Lydia.

Her finger jabbed excitedly at the same location where the other mark had been located. Alex willed himself not to look at the sheriff's mangled, half-burned face and not to inhale the stench of heat and smoke and horrible body smells that emanated from the bag.

He looked at Lydia's finger and the dark, smoke-smudged skin underneath it.

"And look, it's the only bit of his skin that wasn't blackened by the burning," she said excitedly. "That has to mean something." She snapped two more photos of the area.

She was right. The rest of the skin resembled marshmallows that had turned black from too much exposure to a campfire. But not here. This one small area—maybe three inches in diameter—was still pale, normal-looking skin. And running neatly through the center of it was a deep, red mark with smooth edges. Just like Kyle's.

Footsteps sounded in the hallway.

"Quick!" Lydia hissed and started to zip up the bag. "We've got to get him back in there."

As soon as she'd finished, Alex slid the table back into its drawer. His hands were clammy but at least his stomach had stopped twisting.

"Hide," Lydia looked frantically around the room.

Where? The space was like his mother's oversized closet. There was barely room for the body drawers and a shiny, stainless-steel table along with a few small cabinets. Alex assumed these held the tools the doctor—what was he called again? —used to do the autopsies.

"Where?" he said in a loud whisper.

Lydia ducked under the table, then realizing it wouldn't work as a hiding spot, grabbed him and pulled him into the far corner of the room. It was shadowy but visible once whoever opened the door stepped into the room.

Alex heard Lydia breathing too loudly. He wanted to reassure her, but his own heart pumped hard in his chest. The out-of-body experience had faded. Now he recognized his body, but it still felt like he was moving through quicksand or swimming in really weedy water. His brain too felt slow and stupid. Was it a sign of shock? Or—

The door of the morgue swung open with a loud creak. Alex wanted to close his eyes, as though doing so would make him invisible. When he did, he saw Kyle's head again, the crater and mess of whatever was in there oozing. He opened them again quickly.

Katie strode into the room, wrapping her arms around her stomach as she did so. She shivered and glanced around.

"Great hiding spot, guys," she whispered, her voice laced with sarcasm. "We've gotta get out of here. I just left the front desk and the little diversion is over so—"

"Let's go," Alex responded, his voice sounding strangled. This time he was in the lead as their little group filed out the back door of the smelly, cold space and into the warm summer night.

Chapter 15

Jessica Brown

J essica stared at the blinking cursor on the screen. In the past hour, she'd written two sentences. She re-read them for the third time. Two not very good sentences. She deleted, watching all the words disappear. The room had gotten dark. The glow of the laptop's screen was the only light in the cabin. Night came faster up here in the mountains than it did back home. Already the forest was shrouded in blackness, the dark trees silhouetted against the slightly lighter gray-blue sky.

She'd dropped Tony off after their impromptu picnic at the lake and surprised herself by agreeing to meet him early tomorrow for a hike. He wouldn't get them lost, he'd promised with a laugh, and it had made her laugh too. It had felt good. She hadn't realized how little she'd laughed these past few months. Tony was funny, nice, interesting...and she was a complete imbecile for being attracted to him.

Look how it turned out with Bryan, that annoying little voice in her head reminded her. Bryan had taken her heart and not only stepped on it but ground it into the dirty alleyway with his boot for good measure. *What happened to staying single and free? And not putting yourself out there to get emotionally mauled again?*

For months, Jessica had talked herself out of the idea that he was cheating. There were good reasons that he was staying over less often. His work often took him to book shows around the country—sometimes even in other countries—and he was tired after these trips. The fact that he'd stopped inviting her didn't mean he was fooling around. He was just being considerate of her time. He knew she'd had a pressing book tour schedule. And after all, she'd told herself, she knew Bryan. Inside and out.

Or so she'd thought.

It wasn't until she'd found the credit card bill with the purchase at Tiffany's nowhere near her birthday or Christmas that she really started to question other things: the late nights at work, the weekends away—supposedly on guys' golfing trips—that began happening with more regularity. His distractibility when they were together. The way he obsessively checked his phone and popped up from the couch to take "important work calls" more often than ever before.

Still, in her defense, Jessica could say that all these things happened before there had been signs of trouble. She and Bryan were independent people. She'd never minded his trips with friends or the fact that Bryan and she had always maintained separate apartments in the city. But it was the culmination of all the seemingly disparate parts that painted a picture in her mind. Unfortunately, this was months after he'd started sleeping with one of the CEOs at the publishing company where both Jessica and Bryan worked.

Her agent, Theresa, had tut-tutted the company's decision to overlook the dalliance after it had come out. Company policy stated that those in administrative positions were not allowed to have romantic relationships with those in non-administrative roles. Bryan was second in charge of the marketing department.

But seeing as the CEO was the daughter of the company's founder, that was ignored.

Suddenly, it was too hot and stale in the cabin. Jessica needed air. Opening the front door, she let the night wash over her, fresh and cool and delicious smelling. A trillion stars were scattered overhead like someone had spilled a box of sequins. Despite the air, her chest still felt tight. She lowered her head and swung her arms in long, slow circles. She should do yoga tomorrow. Maybe right here on the deck in the morning. It would be beautiful, surrounded by trees and birds. And right after that, she'd take another stab at the manuscript. It would be easier in the morning. Maybe she'd get in a couple of thousand words before she met with Tony for that hike—

A branch snapped in the woods beyond the cabin and Jessica jumped, then laughed at herself. She was still so on-edge, even out here. She'd lived alone for years in the city and had never felt scared. Of course, she also lived in a locked building with a doorman keeping watch all night, every night.

And two people have died since your arrival, that little voice in her head piped up unhelpfully. *And now two more are missing.* Jessica rubbed her hands over her shorts and looked more studiously at the woods. It was impossible to see anything out there. The dark tangle of trees and branches prevented light from penetrating.

The deaths had been accidents, Jessica reminded herself. She'd seen the result of one. There was no reason to suspect anything other than a mishap on an overly treacherous road. As for the boy—well, teens, unfortunately, take risks—it didn't mean that anything more sinister was going on.

But what about the two missing film crew members. Nikki and John? John? No, Joe, Vic had said his name was. She and

Tony had seen Vic again on their way from the lake. He'd looked more disheveled and frustrated. He'd rolled down the window of the old van with a faded decal stating, "Backyard Films" on it.

"That useless deputy wasn't in," he'd said when Jessica asked if there had been any word about the missing people. "But the secretary was. Windbag. She said they're adults and free to come and go as they please."

"So, no search and rescue, huh?" Jessica had asked sympathetically.

Vic snorted. "No."

"We looked around, walked down beyond the point," Tony had said. "But we didn't see anything. I'm sorry."

Vic had shaken his head.

"What will you do now?" Tony had asked.

"Just wait, I guess. I'm going to try hiking up to the tree line, see if I can find any signs of them."

"And you don't think they might have gone to one of the other spots you'll be filming?"

Vic shook his head. "Nah. They'd have told me. Nikki, she's really on top of things, especially communication. She wants to know where everyone is at all times—honestly, it gets annoying—she wouldn't have gone off without letting me know."

"I can help you look some more," Tony had offered, but Vic had waved him off. "It's getting dark. I'm just going to take a quick look around and then…" He'd sighed, looked back toward town. The old van coughed and he'd revved the engine a little. "I might spend the night down here. In the van so I don't miss them. And tomorrow morning," he'd said, his voice strained sounding, "I'm going to tell the deputy that I don't care about them being free to come and go as they please. He needs to do something, you know?" Vic had grunted and swiped a hand over his face, the stubble rasping against his palm. "Thanks for your help," he'd said.

"Please let us know as soon as you hear from them," Jessica added. She jotted down her cell phone number and Tony had scrawled his underneath it. She'd handed the paper to Vic.

"Cell phone reception sucks up here, but texting seems to work. Sometimes."

"Thanks again," Vic had tossed the paper on the dashboard and accelerated toward the small beach.

Had he found Nikki and Joe? Jessica wondered now. Even though he'd said all that stuff about communication, misinterpretations happened all the time. Maybe his crew had gone to check out one of the other film sites after getting footage down at the lake. Or maybe they'd gotten hungry and walked back to town. They could have missed Vic while he was at the sheriff's office, completely unaware that there was a problem.

Snap.

Snap-snap.

The sound of breaking branches jolted Jessica back to the present. She took a step back involuntarily, then another.

"He...hello?" she called out. She'd meant for her voice to sound assertive, but instead, it sounded worried. She cleared her throat. "Who's there?" she called, her voice lower and deeper. "This is private property."

No response.

She was probably telling a raccoon or an opossum that they were trespassing. And anyway—

But then something moved. Barely more than a shadow, a shape drifted from one tree to another. She was sure she'd seen it. Positive it had been upright, on two legs. She squinted, looked harder. A bear? But no, it had been too thin. The profile was much more human than an animal.

Jessica took another step back toward the door, scanning the trees. Where had it gone? She should get inside, but the thought of someone out here, in her private sanctuary, filled her with anger as much as fear. Why should she scurry back into her cabin, be a prisoner in it? If she wanted to stand on the deck and enjoy the stars, then who was this...this intruder to change her mind? In fact, Jessica had a good mind to go back to the cabin, arm herself with some sort of weapon, and come right back out here and—

Another branch broke, then a strange sound filled the air. It was a sort of keening. Goosebumps ran over Jessica's limbs and she stumbled backward toward the cabin.

Chapter 16

loser now.

The shadow moved between the trees, from one to another. Why? Hiding itself among the dark shapes of the overgrown pine and beech trees? Playing games with her? Was there a group of teens out there—maybe classmates of Lydia's—playing a joke on her? Maybe this one had been dared by the others, his or her friends hiding deeper in the cover of the woods.

Jessica straightened her back.

"Hey!" she yelled. "I see you. The game's over. Knock it off and get out of here before I call your parents. Or the police."

The shadow paused. Its outline was still hard to make out in the poor light, but Jessica saw shoulders, the circular shape of a head, and a dark torso. The rest of the body was indistinguishable from the gloomy tree trunks around it.

In the little clump of three pine trees, the strange blueish light glowed faintly. As the figure walked...no glided toward it, Jessica took two more steps back and felt behind her with her hands. She didn't want to turn around, leave her back exposed. Whatever—whoever—it was could rush her, get into the cabin—

The shadowy creature didn't have any interest in her or the cabin though. Instead, it moved toward the light like a moth

127

drawn to a lightbulb. In the blue light, she could see it more clearly. It was tall but stooped and wore a robe, dark and long. Its head seemed too large for its body and at the bottom of its overly long arms, Jessica thought she saw long claws.

She stood transfixed. The shape ignored her completely, its attention fixed on the blue glow that came from the ground. Jessica's breath came in quiet little gasps. This couldn't be real, she told herself, but she couldn't look away. The creature was too large to be a high school kid unless it was on stilts. She should leave and get back inside the cabin, she told herself, to safety. But she was rooted to the deck, her feet paralyzed.

What was it doing? She watched as the figure bent over the blue light. For a second all of its face was dully illuminated. It looked old and gray, streaks of black—or maybe those were deep wrinkles? —lined its face. Its chin was long and pointed like pictures of green Halloween witches and there was a dark mark on its forehead. A cross? No, not quite. Or…yes, it was a cross, but its proportions were all wrong. It was inverted, she realized. An upside-down cross was branded into its high forehead.

Jessica's hands shook as she took two final backward steps toward the door. The knob, slippery under her hands, twisted and she launched herself inside. The figure turned at the sound.

For one horrible second, Jessica saw its eyes. They were eerily white, like glowing bulbs in its face. The twin orbs stared at her and she felt something—some strange sick feeling—pass over her. Then she slammed the door shut and locked it with shaking fingers.

Oh God, oh God! What was she going to do? She was trapped here. She used her weight to shove the kitchen table against the door. What else? She ran across the kitchen and pulled the small free-standing cupboard from its spot. Dry food and a few cans rolled out as she shoved it with all her strength.

The windows!

There were too many of them. He could easily get in one—her heartbeat jackhammered in her chest. Jessica stopped mid-stride, catching herself on a kitchen chair before she lost her balance.

She couldn't stay here. She'd leave, get the hell out of here, and back to town. Sleep in her car or drive all night if she had to. She looked wildly around the room. Where was her purse? The keys? She shook so hard that everything seemed to vibrate.

Could she really have just seen what she thought she did? Or was her mind playing tricks on her? No, it had been real. Real and impossible at the same time.

Keys. Keys!

Where were they?

She'd been leaving them on a little hook by the front door, but a glance told her they weren't there. *Think, Jessica, think. You brought Tony home and came here and then you—did what?*

She pressed her fingers against her eyes as though she could manually make them remember where she'd last seen the keys. And then, like magic, she did.

The table. She'd tossed them on the table when she'd walked in. With the leftovers from dinner. She ran to the table, threw aside the plastic bag with the leftover food and napkins. A stack of papers lay under that. Tony had given her copies he'd made at the library—the history of this place. She pushed them aside. Silver glinted underneath.

Clutching the keys tightly, she shoved the cabinet and then the table back away from the door and ran over her bare toes in the process. She yelped and hopped on one foot, unlocking the bolt while shoving the table further back with her hip. Her toes felt like she'd dropped a burning log onto them. Backtracking, she snagged her purse and looped it over her arm.

Keys in hand, Jessica prepared to run to the car. She'd locked it—a force of habit…but what if whatever he was—was already in her vehicle? Maybe it could go through doors. Images of horror movies she'd seen as a teen flickered across her brain. She pictured herself driving down the steep, winding road and then seeing that gray face and those white, bulging eyes in the rearview mirror—

Jessica sagged against the door. What other choice did she have? Stay here and have him come through a window? Or a door? He could walk through walls for all she knew. A burst of hysterical laughter erupted from her mouth.

She couldn't stay here. Better to take her chances out in the open. Jessica opened the door but then slammed it shut. Ran to the kitchen and grabbed the biggest, sharpest-looking knife from the bunch, and held it out in front of her. In her other hand, she gripped her key fob.

Ready.

She opened the door again and slipped out onto the deck. Instantly, she wished she'd also brought a flashlight. Smudges of dark clouds had rolled in, blotting out most of the stars and the three-quarter moon. Jessica's heartbeat pounded in her ears. She looked toward the little grove of pine trees.

There was nothing there.

No light.

No figure.

Nothing.

She paused momentarily relieved. Maybe he'd gone. Maybe she'd fallen asleep on the couch and been dreaming. Maybe—

Oh, shut up.

Jessica plunged through the darkness. Her feet slapped painfully over the gravel. There was no other sound in the night around her. Even the frogs and crickets had fallen silent. Jessica heard only her ragged breath and the stones underfoot.

Almost there.

Just a few more steps.

She hit the unlock button, realizing too late that it would have lit her path, at least for a few precious seconds.

Someone was inside the vehicle. A dark figure hunched over the steering wheel. Jessica swallowed down the scream in her throat. She wavered, then turned back toward the house. There was movement from the corner of her eye. She looked wildly toward the grove of pines.

No.

That wasn't possible.

Jessica blinked but he was still there. She could just make out the bent figure, the dark robes. But how—how could it be in two places at once?

Halfway back to the cabin, Jessica stopped. What—could he teleport himself? Take more than one figure simultaneously? Another bit of panicked laughter bubbled up in her chest like a fizzy glass of champagne. Turning yet again, she ran back to the car. He couldn't be in there now, not if she'd just seen him in the trees. He couldn't—

Her hand closed over the door handle. She yanked it open, held the knife high in her other hand. Her arm shook. Time stopped as she waited to see the sickly gray face, and bulging fish eyes staring back at her.

But the seat was empty. Except for her windbreaker, which she'd left over the back of it. Not the figure's hulking shape, but a stupid jacket. A strangled half-laugh-half-cry erupted from her throat, and she threw herself behind the wheel. Slammed the door shut. Looking wildly back toward the blueish light and the pine trees, Jessica could see that the figure was still there. Its face was light with a dull bluish glow and its lips were moving as the body gently swayed.

Jessica jerked the shifter into reverse, turned the key, and slammed on the gas. Gravel spewed under the tires as she backed up wildly, did a three-point turn on the grass, and raced down the driveway.

Safe.

She was safe.

Wasn't she?

Jessica kept an eye on the rearview mirror all the way into town and kept her foot firmly down on the gas pedal.

Chapter 17

Vic Mellin

Vic sighed and rubbed a hand over his face, his palm smooth against sandpaper cheeks. It was late and he'd been at this for hours. He rubbed his eyes next, the lids gritty. Opening them wide, he looked yet again at the film footage of the area. It had been only a few days since his arrival, but it felt like months. He'd retreated to his hotel room, hoping that any minute Nikki and Joe would walk through the door, exhausted but otherwise fine with some harebrained story to tell about their impromptu disappearance. They'd gotten misplaced in the forest. They'd capsized a kayak and had gotten disoriented. He'd been waiting for the same thing to happen for hours though and so far...nothing.

Vic sighed and scanned ahead in the footage. There were hours and hours of it, most of which would never be used. He stopped when a section he hadn't reviewed yet came into focus: the crash down at Gargun's Footstool. The quality was pretty good considering the light had been less-than-ideal. The wreckage was still smoldering in the shot, and it immediately brought back the horrible scent of burning plastic and melting metal...and human flesh? He pushed the last thought away and studied the surrounding areas. The cliffs were as jagged as ever, their dull, dark rock rising sinisterly from the tangled undergrowth nearer the lake. At this angle, they looked like teeth, as though a dragon or other monster had its mouth wide open, its maw pointed toward the sky.

The filming wasn't half bad, even Joe would have to agree to that. Vic had kept a steady hand and the lens panned from one end of the crash site to the other, then back again. He leaned in, studied the next shot. He'd taken a slightly wider angle there, getting more of the cliff face. This had been where he'd seen that movement up on the cliff and—

Hang on.

What was that? Vic hit a button and reversed the video, paused, and restarted it in slow-mo. There had been something there that didn't fit: a shape or shadow…somewhere higher up from the crash and to the right. He slowed the film down even further as the time signature on the video drew close.

There.

Half peeking out of the side of the cliff was a man. Or an animal? Vic squinted. No, it was a human form. What the hell would someone be doing up there? And how—Vic froze the image—how was he maintaining his balance on the jagged edges of the cliff? Maybe a rock climber? But why wouldn't they have said anything, called out to him? And why would you continue climbing there if you'd seen the crash?

His heart thudded harder in his chest.

Someone had seen it happen. Someone else was a witness… but who?

Vic zoomed in. The frame became so large on the laptop that it started to pixelate, growing fuzzy. He stared.

Blinked and shook his head.

Impossible.

What he was seeing on the screen...that couldn't be real.

A gray figure shrouded in a dark, black cloak that was tattered and frayed around the edges. It was hunched but stood—seemed to float—slightly above a stone outcropping. Vic swallowed and tasted the onions from the roast beef sub he'd eaten mindlessly an hour earlier.

A mixture of excitement and dread filled him. He clicked a button, let the film continue in slow motion. The figure swung its head in slow jerky motions toward the camera's lens. Its face was dark gray—nearly the same color as the stone around it—but it was the thing's eyes that made Vic's stomach tighten. They were pure white and bulged outward like oversized goldfish eyes.

Vic leaned back in the uncomfortable desk chair, his hand over his mouth and chin, and struggled to find reasonable explanations to quell the burble of excitement tingling in his hands. There could be a reasonable explanation: someone messing around, dressed up in a costume. A kid playing a prank. An animal that...

Just stop. His brain said quietly. Just stop. None of that makes sense.

But what did?

That he'd caught an image of the gargun? That it was not only real but supernatural—able to move around not by walking but by...by floating? Vic shoved the chair back. He paced the room, rubbed a hand over the back of his neck.

What did this mean? Was it enough to work with? If only the shot was clearer. And longer. Still, he'd gotten it. He'd captured footage of a very real creature. This would change everything for him! For Backyard Films...imagine what this meant? Vic could already see himself being interviewed by other, bigger filmmakers. Finally. Finally, he'd gotten his lucky break.

He wanted to whoop and jump around the room, pump a fist in the air. He'd done it—somehow caught an image of the gargun…it was real. Not only real but out there at Stillwater Lake. At least it had been. He tried to do the math quickly—how long since he'd been there and gotten this footage? But his brain was like mush. He paced, held his head in his hands as though he could squeeze the information out of it.

He stopped pacing.

Where had it gone? Did it live there?

Vic scrambled to the bed where he'd hauled in a few equipment bags from the van. He rummaged through, looking for the black binder. Most of the research the team had done had been online. Knowing the internet connection out here would be spotty, Nikki—ever-efficient—had put together a project binder on the history of the gargun. This was mostly for Vic's benefit as he'd use the notes and clippings to prepare his narratives.

He pulled cables and cords out of the first bag, an extra bottle of sunscreen and bug repellant tucked into a zippered gallon bag, a second, older laptop, and an extra couple of tripods. Finally, toward the bottom, Vic felt the smooth, cool surface of the binder.

Jerking it out, he flipped through the plastic-covered pages. Nikki had carefully compiled any information Vic found, along with her extensive research and notes, and neatly labeled everything for easy access on the road.

The tabs read: "Amenities," "Potential Locations," "Maps," "Timeline," and lastly, "History". He flipped to that one. The plastic pages slapped together, reminding him of the bubble-gum-scented baseball cards he'd collected as a kid.

"History and notes of the gargun," the tabbed divider said in Nikki's neat, squarish handwriting. Vic flipped over the general information that they'd gathered about the habits of the gargun and the area's folklore to the sections pulled from Vermont-authored books on the subject.

"Local legend has it that the gargun is one of three things," a section of the text pulled from a book called, *Monsters in the Green Mountains: Fact or Fable?* noted. "That it's a monster similar to Vermont's well-known, 'Champ,' or the famous Loch Ness of Scotland; that it is a Native American story come to life; or that it is a demonic or ghostly presence tied to the area of Stillwater Lake from the time the town was first formed.

"Vermonters themselves are divided on the history of the creature, with many not believing in its presence at all. Still, among those faithful to the idea, a greater ratio believes that not only is the monster real but that its history is entwined with the town's own. The presence of a ghostly or demonic force in the area has been written about infrequently. That, however, is believed to be due to superstitions regarding the town's checkered history."

Vic swallowed and paused, hesitant to read more. Though he'd started Backyard Films to research unexplained phenomena that happened, "right in your backyard," he'd never believed the mysteries. Guy had been the partner fully vested in the spiritual or metaphysical side of the stories the company covered. Vic had been more interested in the business end of things: the profit potential helped him approve or discourage Guy's different interests. And boxing and selling folklore and tall tales to an audience were for entertainment purposes only, in his mind anyway. He couldn't help it if some nut job really believed in Bigfoot or pigmen or the gargun for that matter.

Vic thought of himself as a businessman first and foremost and an investigative reporter along with the face of Backyard Films—second.

Flipping forward, Vic skimmed the next pages of text. The information was discombobulating: the creature was supposedly hairy, not smooth-skinned. It walked upright—no, it crawled on all fours. Half of the problem proving some of these things existed was the fact that everyone who had supposedly seen them, reported different things. Another reason, Vic had always told Guy, not to believe in what you couldn't see yourself.

"...gray in appearance, with bulging, frog-like eyes." The bit of text popped off the page as though it were highlighted in neon green. Vic bent his head closer, his own tired eyes squinting to make out the text.

"Mrs. Hershel stated that the gray figure approached her front door, then veered off into the trees," a newspaper article from 1971 stated. 'It didn't look human,' she reported. 'Its skin was gray and its face was lined. But it was the eyes—' Mrs. Hershel at this point broke into sobs and the interview was discontinued.

"This, of course, is just one of the many sightings of the gargun that have taken place in the Stillwater Lake area over the years. Always around the same time of the year—the midsummer—and always close to the lake or other haunts of the town's founding fathers."

The article ended there, and Vic stood suddenly. The binder dropped onto the mattress.

He had to get out of here. The room felt like it was contracting, growing smaller and hotter and he needed some air. Vic grabbed the room key and pulled the locked door shut hard behind him. He strode across the crowded parking lot. The little motel was filled to capacity and this late at night nearly every parking spot was full.

The summer air was balmy and fresh after the stale room air though. He sucked in a few big breaths, rolled his shoulders, and walked. A little space. He needed a little space to clear his head, to think things through. Figure out what to do next.

And then?

A drink. That's what Vic needed. A tall, stiff drink. His mouth watered just thinking about it.

He loped along, ignored the scattered stars overhead and the way that the breeze playfully tugged at the collar of his shirt. Would the grocery store carry liquor? No, but he remembered suddenly the small gas station just down the street. It had a miniature-sized liquor outlet in it. He walked in that direction, so caught up in his thoughts that he was startled when he heard a voice near an overgrown lilac bush outside the general store.

"...have to let someone know. This could put the deputy and other people looking into the deaths in danger!" a girl's voice rose and someone else in the group shushed her.

"Sorry. But—"

"No one is going to believe us," another voice said, this one deeper. "I mean, can you picture it? 'Hey Deputy Pepper, guess what? We found the gargun's mark on the bodies of the two people who just died. You might want to look into that.'" The voice broke off with a snort. "It sounds crazy."

"It is crazy," the first voice chimed in. "But that doesn't mean it's untrue."

Vic hadn't realized he'd come to a complete stop until he heard another voice—a third—shushing the first two.

There was a second of silence, then, "Um, hello, can we help you?" A dark-haired girl pulled back from the shadowy canopy

139

of leaves and stared hostilely at Vic.

"Oh, sorry, guys. I didn't mean to interrupt," Vic used his smooth TV voice. "I...well." He took a couple of steps closer and chuckled. "I couldn't help overhearing."

"What did you hear?" another girl asked. He couldn't see her face, but her voice sounded pinched and nervous.

"Nothing much. Something about marks and bodies." He tried to make it sound like he was nervous. "Sorry again." He moved as though he were leaving. Took a few steps and then stopped, frowned, and turned back toward them. "I'm from out of town—a filmmaker. Here to do a documentary on the gargun. And you guys wouldn't believe what I just saw in some footage I got earlier this week at Gargun's Footstool. When you'd mentioned, uh, the marks you saw...pardon my asking, but they wouldn't have been on a victim of the car accident, would they?"

The male voice cursed under his breath but the girl who'd been hidden by the shadows stepped forward cautiously. Her pale hair was tied into a messy bun and her thin arms were so white they nearly glowed in the moonlight.

"You're Mr. Mellin, aren't you?" she asked.

Vic nodded. She looked vaguely familiar—short with an upturned nose and clear, serious eyes.

"I'm Lydia. You talked with my mother about renting a cabin from us?"

Vic nodded again, remembering the young woman who'd stood behind the tall desk at the property rental place.

"Yeah, that's right. I remember you. Any cabins open up?" he joked.

A brief smile flitted over Lydia's face. "No, sorry."

"I was kidding," Vic let a moment of silence pass and then

140

cleared his throat. "But not about what I saw down on the cliffs."

The teenage boy stepped forward. Tall and sinewy with a mop of brownish curls he sported a dark tan and vaguely resembled an A-list celebrity who Vic couldn't remember the name of.

"What did you see?" the kid asked.

Vic weighed his options. He wanted to know more about this mark that the kids had been talking about. He wanted to know more about the history of the gargun here in this place, from the people who lived here.

And honestly, he wanted to show someone else—anyone else—the video feed. He wasn't yet ready to bring it to the sheriff's office. Especially since the staff had made light of the fact that Nikki and Joe were missing. But the need to tell someone—anyone—was greater than his instinct to not confide in a bunch of kids. Besides, what if the gargun was real? What if that's what he'd caught on camera?

"I think I saw the gargun," Vic said finally.

The girl, Lydia, sucked in a breath and looked at the boy. He frowned but nodded.

"Let's go take a look," he said.

Chapter 18

Tony Bradford

Tony woke to a pounding noise. For one bleary moment he thought he was back in Boston, the jackhammer at the construction site across the street was going again. But then he remembered where he was. Someone pounded at the cabin's door.

He glanced at the clock as he pulled a pair of shorts over his boxers. Just after one in the morning. He flicked on the lights in the living room as he walked through and opened the door a crack.

Jessica stood on the top step, her hair and eyes wild.

"Please, let me in." She put a hand through the narrow slot as though she expected him to slam the door in her face. Instead, he opened it wide, and she ducked inside.

"Close it. Close it." She was shaking, her whole body trembling. Her skin was an unnatural shade of white.

"What happened?" Tony asked. "Are you okay?"

She shook her head, then nodded.

"Yes, I think so. I mean, I'm not hurt just…just scared out of my wits."

Tony took her hand and led her to the living room. It was

a small cabin with an open floor plan, other than the small bedroom which was tucked along the eaves. He settled Jessica onto the blue couch and retrieved a bottle of scotch and two glasses from the kitchen.

"Here, drink this." He handed her a glass filled a quarter full. She thanked him and tossed it back in one gulp.

He sat on the chair opposite her and raised his eyebrows.

"Another?"

She nodded.

He refilled the glass and handed it to her. She didn't gulp it this time but still managed to get three sips in while Tony had his first. He smiled at her tentatively, setting his glass on the table between them.

"Are you okay?" he asked again. He'd grabbed a T-shirt off the chair in the kitchen and pulled it on.

"Yes. Thank you. That—" she nodded toward her glass—"helped."

She looked better, her color slowly returning, and the violent shaking had turned into more of a gentle tremble.

"Can I get you anything else? A blanket? Sweatshirt?"

"No, thank you. I'm fine." She gave a half laugh but it sounded strangled. "I'm sorry to barge in here like this in the middle of the night. I just...I just didn't know where else to go." She put her hands over her face and spoke through her fingers. "Half of me wanted to just keep driving, back to the city. Another half of me still thinks I dreamed it all."

Tony wanted to ask, "All of what?" but refrained. He'd worked as the assistant hospital chaplain during divinity school and had learned early on that people needed time to process things: grief, anger, fear. It was better to wait until the person was ready to speak, rather than rush them.

They sat in silence for a few minutes, then Jessica lowered her nearly empty glass to the table and let out a sigh.

"Thank you. I'm sorry again for—"

"Don't," Tony said. "I'm glad you didn't head back to the city. And that you felt comfortable enough with me to come here."

She met his eyes, smiled slightly. "You're easy to talk to." She shook her head. "I think I might be losing my mind. Have you ever seen something that you know can't be real? Like, you'd swear you were dreaming because there is absolutely no other plausible explanation?"

She paused, looked at Tony.

He nodded.

"I saw—" she stopped, bit her lip.

"A ghost?" Tony half-smiled.

She shook her head. "No. I don't believe in ghosts."

"That makes two of us."

"But I don't believe in what I just saw either," she glanced toward the door. "I saw a…a creature, Tony. I think it was the…" Jessica paused, looked from him to the door and back again as though expecting whatever it was to walk through. "The gargun." She reached for her glass again and drained it.

Tony's heart missed a single beat before it resumed its regular rhythm.

"Where?"

"At my cabin. Well, outside it. I know how it sounds but I swear I'm not making it up, not imagining it. It…it came out of the woods. I was outdoors, getting some fresh air. And it came right out of the trees. It walked—it walked to this little grove of pine trees. And there was a strange bluish light coming from there. I—I saw it the other night, too. The light I mean, not the—the gargun."

Tony remembered the day they'd met. How distracted Jessica had been and how she'd kept looking at the little grove of pine trees.

"And then what?"

She looked from her empty glass to him.

"Then—nothing. I mean, I thought he was going to come for me, you know? I was so scared. Paralyzed really," she shivered and wrapped her arms around herself. Tony reached under the coffee table and pulled a fuzzy plaid blanket out of a basket there and spread it over her.

"Thanks," she murmured. She closed her eyes.

"I was on the deck. He was in the trees and seemed to be just sort of staring downward, at the light. I started to run for my car, but then thought he'd gotten into it somehow. He hadn't, it was just my jacket on the seat. I had to get out. Had to leave. I don't want to go back there. Not ever." She shook her head, pulled the blanket up to her chin.

"Did he say anything?"

Jessica shook her head. "No."

Tony nodded, leaned forward with his arms resting on his knees.

"Do you want me to go back? Have a look around?"

She shook her head again, violently this time.

"No, please don't. Maybe tomorrow. In the morning—we can go together." Her eyes looked heavy. "I still need to get my things. And I'm not sure where else I can go. Maybe there's a room empty at a B&B or that little motel in town."

Tony nodded but doubted with all the visitors and the festival starting tomorrow she'd have much luck finding anything. *She could stay here,* a little voice whispered in his brain. *That's what you've been imagining anyway, isn't it?* He stood up.

145

"We can go back in the morning after everything has…has calmed down. We'll take a look around. If you're still feeling uneasy being there, maybe you and I could switch cabins. Or Penny might know someone—somewhere else you could stay. But for tonight you're welcome to stay here. I'll put fresh sheets on the bed and take the couch. You'll be—"

"No, no, I can't." Jessica's voice was firm. "Thank you, Tony, but I feel bad enough about all of this already. I'll sleep right here on the couch if you don't mind. I don't snore—at least, I'm pretty sure I don't."

Tony smiled.

"And I'm still so keyed up that I doubt I'll get much sleep anyway." She stifled a yawn and gave him a half-smile.

He began to protest but she shook her head again adamantly.

"Really, please. I just feel better being here."

"If you're sure," he said.

She nodded. "Definitely. But I will take you up on your offer to go back to the cabin in the morning with me. I—I'd rather not have to do that on my own."

He nodded. "Sure."

Tony gathered the glasses, asked if she wanted another blanket or an extra pillow. She didn't. As he flicked the lights off, he glanced at her again. Her cheeks were pink and her eyes, despite what she'd said about being unable to sleep, looked droopy.

Chapter 19

Tony Bradford

Tony half-woke to the sound of someone shuffling to the bathroom. He dozed again and then heard the creak of feet moving into the kitchen. Jessica was up. He tried to untangle himself from the dream he'd been having—something to do with a wolf-like creature following him in the forest—but failed.

The next time he opened his eyes, dull gray light filtered in through the bedroom window. He'd forgotten to shut the curtains last night. He groaned and flipped onto his back, slowly stretching his arms and legs.

He smelled coffee as he fumbled with the clock on the bedside table. It was just after seven.

"Sorry, did I wake you?" Jessica asked when he emerged from the bedroom. She was curled on the wingchair by the cold fireplace. Even dressed in her wrinkled clothes from the night before she looked lovely, Tony thought. She was flipping through one of the books of folklore Tony had brought with him but stood as he came into the room. She went to the kitchen and returned with a steaming mug of coffee in hand.

"Coffee?"

147

"Sure, thanks," he said and took the mug gratefully. His fingers brushed against hers and she smiled. He tried to ignore the electric current running up his arm. *Meredith. Meredith. Meredith.*

"I didn't see cream in the fridge so assume you drink it without?"

Tony nodded. "Just black. Find anything enlightening in there?" he looked at the stack of books, glad for a distraction. He'd brought an embarrassing number of them with him, most of his collection. He sipped his coffee, the acrid taste welcome, and tried to squash his embarrassment at Jessica finding the books. Not that it was secret—he'd left the stack on the side table. But then, he hadn't expected visitors.

"Yes, actually. Lots of interesting stuff. It's funny, I never considered the possibility that some of these legends might be real. To me they've always been a little, well," she cleared her throat and glanced apologetically toward Tony.

"Crazy?" he offered.

She smiled. "Yeah. But after last night...Well. I'm a little more open to the idea."

They chatted for a few more minutes, about their lives in the city, and what they loved and hated about it. He told her more than he'd intended about his work—how he'd been struggling for some time, unsure if he wanted to keep doing the work he had been. It was stressful and in the last several months, he'd found it more difficult than rewarding.

"But I'm not sure I'm ready to move on. What would I do if I changed careers?" Tony sipped the rest of his coffee that had gone cold.

He glanced at the carved wooden clock on the wall. It was past nine.

"I didn't realize it had gotten so late. You're too easy to talk to." He smiled and put his hand out for her empty mug. Instead, Jessica slipped her fingers into his.

"It was nice listening to someone else's problems for a change. One of the downsides of living and working by yourself is that you have a lot of time to listen to your own problems. This was a nice break."

A smile tugged up the corner of his lips. "Glad to help." He squeezed her hand. "Jessica, there's something I need to tell you. Should have told you before."

Her eyes widened. "You're not married, are you?" Jessica pulled her hand free. Tony's instantly felt cold.

Tony shook his head. "No. But I have been in a long-term relationship. We're..." he glanced out the window without really seeing anything. "We're taking a break. To be completely honest, I suggested we have some time apart because I think we want different things."

"She wants..." Jessica paused. "To get married? Have kids?"

"Yeah."

"And you don't."

"No. No, I mean I do want those things. And Meredith and I—we should be perfect together. On paper, we are perfect together. Same values. Same interests. Same backgrounds. But it's like there's a problem with all that sameness. Do you know what I mean?"

Jessica nodded. "Yes."

"You do?" Tony hadn't expected that.

"My ex and I—Bryan—we were perfect together too. Everyone said so. We were interested in similar things—okay, not golf, but mostly we liked to do the same things. We were both in publishing too, so moved in the same circles there. We even shared a workplace, for pity's sake. But we weren't good together underneath it all. We were just different people, you know? I blame him," she chuckled dryly and Tony smiled.

He felt like he was at the top of a high cliff, staring over the edge. Before he could stop himself he said, "I feel...something for you."

Jessica stared at him intently.

"I have no idea if we'd be good together. And I don't know if you're even interested in finding out—"

Jessica reached back across the table and gripped his hand, her fingers tight and warm in his.

"I'd like to."

Tony felt like sparklers had ignited in his chest. He couldn't help grinning.

"Really?"

"Yes."

He leaned across the table and cupped a hand around her cheek. It was soft, her skin velvety.

"Can I kiss you?"

She smiled. "That's very old-fashioned of you, Mr. Bradford."

"Oh, you have no idea how old-fashioned I am, Ms. Brown. I hope that won't be a problem."

She drew closer and Tony could see that her dark blue eyes were rimmed in navy.

"Yes," she whispered.

"Yes, what?" His heartbeat thudded loudly in his head.

"Yes, you can kiss me."

Tony took his time, tracing the line of her lips with his eyes before leaning in and giving her a slow, gentle kiss. The sparklers in his belly turned into fireworks explosions and when he drew back, Jessica was smiling.

"Wow."

"That's what I was going to say."

They sat in silence for a few seconds, the sound of birds outside the windows the only noise. Then Tony cleared his throat and slid his hand over hers.

"I hate to break the mood, but do you want to go back to your cabin now and have a look around?"

Jessica shivered but nodded.

"We could drive over and chat with Penny first. See if she has something else. Or do you want to try your luck at the motel? My offer to switch cabins is still on the table too, if you want."

"No, thank you. I feel bad enough I ruined a night of your sleep—"

He started to protest, but she smiled, putting a finger over his lips.

"I'll go and see Penny after we've been to the cabin. I'll feel better once we've looked around."

***

Jessica's cabin looked very much as it had the first time Tony had seen it. Flowers fluttered in a hot breeze and the exterior trim was slightly faded, in need of a fresh coat of paint. The windows and curtains were still drawn from the night before.

"Should we look inside first?"

Jessica nodded. They walked through all the rooms together. Jessica's half-finished cup of tea was still on a side table in the living room, next to a scattering of magazines. The kitchen was slightly messy and Jessica, seemingly embarrassed by her housekeeping skills, explained that she'd pushed some furniture around the night before. Tony wanted to laugh but kept a

straight face as she hurriedly collected the clothes strewn over
the furniture and floor and stuffed them in an empty bag on the
kitchen counter. The loft bedroom featured a saggy-looking
queen-sized bed that was unmade. More clothes had been left
in clumps around the floor. It and the tiny bathroom were
empty.

"Nothing hiding under here," Tony stood after looking beneath the bed. "Want me to check the closet?"

"No, that's okay." Jessica walked over and threw the door
open. She poked around the small space and shook her head.
"All clear."

She laughed suddenly.

"I feel like I'm five years old again and my parents are checking
to make sure no monsters are hiding anywhere."

Tony smiled. "They sound like good parents."

"Yes, they were."

"Are you still close?"

Jessica paused with the closet door partially closed. "They
died several years ago in a boating accident overseas."

Tony's felt stupid, wished he could take the question back.
"That must have been hard."

"It was," she sighed, her eyes looking suddenly tired. "It was
good that I had…" her voice drifted off momentarily. "My
work."

She cleared her throat and motioned toward the downstairs.
"We should probably check outside."

They trooped back down the winding wrought iron staircase
and walked back toward the front door. Tony noticed a high-
end laptop on the kitchen table, and several pages spread out
around it. The top one said in big, bold letters: *Lovely Beginnings*
by Claudia Snow.

Claudia Snow? Tony's stomach did a weird clenching thing. The Claudia Snow? World-famous author...and he was standing in her kitchen right now? He couldn't help but look at her. He hadn't read her books, but he'd heard her name enough to know that she was hugely popular. She wrote women's fiction, right? Was it romance?

"Oh, uh," Jessica reached around Tony and shuffled the pages together, placing them face down on the table. She forced a laugh. "Guess my secret's out."

"Claudia Snow—I can't believe it. My mother loves your books. In fact, she got her whole book club turned on to you," Tony said. "Romance novels, right?"

"Family drama..." Jessica started to say but then stopped. "Yes. Romance. Bodice rippers, I guess you'd say, with a time travel angle."

Tony still felt a little stunned. It's not that he was easily impressed, at least, not usually. He'd met his share of rich and powerful people, famous people in the work he did. But not anyone as well known as Claudia. Or Jessica rather.

"How long have you been writing?"

"Since I could hold a pencil. My mother said even before that, I'd make up stories and tell them to her while I took baths."

"That's amazing, to be passionate about something for so long. Do you still love it?"

Jessica paused her hand on the doorknob. Her eyes had turned a darker shade. Tony wasn't sure if it was because she'd been embarrassed to be found out or if it was discussing her work life.

"I used to. It's all...well. It's all gotten a little complicated lately. I had...personal trouble that's left me blocked. The truth is, I haven't written for months. I'm not sure if I can again.

That's why I came up here. To get away and let my muse run free. Only I'm afraid instead she's run away."

Her face was sad suddenly and Tony wished he hadn't asked, hadn't even seen the papers. She was different now. She seemed younger and more vulnerable. Less the sophisticated big city woman in charge and more like a flawed, hurt human. She'd lost her parents and now her love of writing—it must have been scary, having everything you depended on fall away from you.

He was about to say so when she pulled the front door open. Her face was once again serene and he wondered how she did it—turned off her emotions like that. He'd never been good at it. Whatever Tony felt was spread clearly across his face. Tony followed her out onto the hot deck. Sunlight streamed down and the flowers were already starting to wilt.

"Let's check the grove of pines next," Jessica seemed in a hurry to change the subject and Tony didn't try to stop her. He was here on sabbatical and appreciated the fact that no one here cared about the work that consumed him back home. If Jessica was looking for a little peace and quiet, time to reflect and be inspired, he wasn't going to be the one to ruin it for her.

"Good idea."

They walked in unison to the little grove of pine trees, Jessica easily keeping up with his long stride. What had looked like three trees was five, so tightly twisted together, their branches overlapped, making it nearly impossible to tell where one ended and another began. Tony bent low near the trunks hoping to see something in the soil under the trees. A discarded flashlight, a bug zapper, or a solar light—something to make sense of the blueish glow that Jessica had described.

But there was nothing, just a pile of old pine needles that had turned orange. Nearby a bird's nest was crumpled in the grass.

Tony glanced at Jessica. She frowned at the earth, as though she too had been hoping for a miraculous find.

"I'll get a shovel," Jessica said. "I saw one in the backyard the other day, leaning up on the little storage shed. Whatever is making that light—it must be coming from here."

"Let me." Tony retrieved the shovel which had seen better days. The earth was damp and turned easily under it. A few minutes later, he had carved out a hole about two feet in length. Using the tip of the shovel, he poked around in the loose soil.

There was nothing. Occasionally, the shovel's tip clanged against a small stone submerged in the ground, but nothing large. He jabbed the earth again with the shovel's tip and then—*clang*.

Much too loud for a small stone.

"It could be a larger rock," he told Jessica but hoped it wasn't. Using the tip of the shovel, he tested soil around the spot, hitting something over and over, the shovel's pointed edge connecting with something else that was metal.

After dragging up a few shovelfuls of soil, Tony squatted, and Jessica followed suit. Tossing the shovel aside, they glanced at each other, then plunged their hands into the dirt with grins. Brushing away loose soil, they uncovered an object. It was small, about the size of a shoebox, and felt like metal.

"What do you think it is?" Jessica breathed, her mouth close to his ear. The hair on the back of his neck stood up.

"I don't know. Let's get it out of there and have a look."

They pulled the box out of the earth.

"If there had been a label it's gone now," Jessica said.

Tony grunted slightly as the last corner of the box came free. They placed it gently on the ground between them.

"You should do the honors," Tony said.

Jessica nodded and used both hands to tug the cover, while Tony held onto the bottom. There was a loud shriek as the metal rubbed against metal and then the lid came off. Jessica peered inside, Tony looking over her shoulder. Inside the box was a packet wrapped in cloth. It was moldy and mildewed. The smell coming from the box was strong and musty.

Jessica grabbed the material and pulled it upward. Beneath the old fabric was a book with an oilskin cover. It seemed in surprisingly good shape, the pages along the edge yellowed but still intact.

"What do you think it is?" Jessica asked. Already, she'd flipped open the cover.

"Contract and bill of sale," the first page read in faded red ink. Underneath it were columns and rows of barely visible black ink.

"Looks like a ledger."

Under the first heading was neatly printed: "Goods gained," and under the second: "Date". The third column stated: "Payment received". Half of the page was filled with handwritten numbers under the first column: each with initials to go along with them. The first entry stated "#1: H.B." On the second line, it read, "#2: BG." On the line below that "#3: EK," was recorded.

"A list of goods purchased?" Tony asked. "I wonder why that was so important to bury?"

"There must be a reason. Maybe it's why the gargun keeps returning to this spot."

She traced her finger down the first row and then froze.

"That's impossible. Look," her voice was little more than a horrified whisper. "Look at this date, Tony."

He looked. A strange feeling started in his chest like a vice had squeezed out all the oxygen, leaving him only a straw to breathe with.

"That's this week," he said. "But how—"

"I don't know." Jessica's voice shook and so did her hands. "And look at the initials."

The lines toward the middle of the page were written in darker ink. Clearly, Tony could see the initials: "RR," followed by "KL".

"What was the sheriff's first name?" Jessica's voice was hoarse.

"I'm not sure. But his last name was Rinko."

"And the boy—the teenager who had the accident...could he have been KL?"

Tony felt the trees around him grow closer. It was suddenly excessively hot and hard to breathe. Jessica looked like she was struggling too, her face had gone ghostly pale again and her eyes were wide. The hand holding the ledger shook so hard Tony expected her to drop it.

"I'm not sure. We don't know what this means—"

"I think we should take it to someone. The police—someone who can help." She looked at him a little wildly.

Tony doubted that the deputy or anyone else in charge would have any ideas how this box, buried in the undisturbed ground, could have information from this week. It didn't make any sense. But he nodded dumbly. It was her cabin after all, and her idea to dig here. He imagined the scene: he and Jessica marching into the small police office bearing a book they'd found in the ground, insisting that not only was it the gargun's but that it was using it to...to what? Keep a record of the names and dates of the people it killed?

Chapter 20

Vic Mellin

I t was cramped in Vic's motel room, the three teens sprawled on the beds while Vic stood by his laptop on the desk. He thought about how this would sound in the newspaper. "45-year-old filmmaker lures teens to a motel room," but shrugged the thought away. He hadn't had to do much luring, after all. The kids were here of their own free will. And Vic was just happy he had other people to confirm what he'd seen in the video feed.

"It's coming up now," he said quietly, and all three kids leaned toward the screen. The boy stood up, got close, and hovered over the empty desk chair.

Vic watched the screen and then the kids' faces like it was a ping pong tournament. As soon as the creature appeared on the screen, he felt a wave of relief. The blonde girl—Lydia—gasped and covered her mouth with her hands. The other girl's eyes went wide, and the boy cursed, then ran a hand roughly through his hair.

"Is that what you saw down there, Alex?" Lydia asked.

The kid shook his head. "I don't know. It was too dark to see much."

"Wait, what?" the dark-haired girl, Katie, asked. "You saw the gargun? Where? At Gargun's Footstool?"

"Yeah. Well, no," Alex said a little too quickly. "But I heard something. When I was down there with Kyle."

Katie gave him a small kick. "You should have told me."

She glanced at Vic, seeming to remember they weren't alone in the room.

"Look, forget I said that all right?" Alex said.

"Forgotten," Vic said.

"Can we see it again?" Lydia asked. The screen had returned to panning the cliff's face.

"Sure." Vic backed up the film to the right spot. He looked at the screen again, watching with the kids, hoping in some illogical way that this time they wouldn't see the creature. That the dark face would end up just being part of the rock, that the black cloak would end up just being shadows.

But the pale orbs in the thing's face made that wish impossible.

"It's like it has shark eyes," Lydia said with a shiver. "They look so...so dead."

"They're too bulgy to be a shark's," Katie said. "These are more like, I don't know. Fish or frog eyes or something."

Alex continued to stare at the screen, his mouth partially open. I know, kid, I know, Vic wanted to say. He couldn't believe it was real either.

"I think it may have taken members of my crew," Vic blurted out, breaking the silence in the room. "They went missing and I think that that thing—" he jabbed a finger at the screen. "Got them."

All three sets of eyes stared at him.

"Woah," Alex said. "When did that happen?"

"Earlier today. I left them down at the lake and then they

disappeared. Poof, like gone, gone, you know? The sheriff's office doesn't think it's a big deal. Thinks they just went off to another area, that we miscommunicated. But I don't think so." Vic lowered his voice, looked from one set of eyes to another. "We had plans to check out some more of the filming locations, but they wouldn't leave without telling me."

"So, you think what? That the gargun killed them?" Katie asked. The thick eyeliner gave her a slightly ghoulish look.

Vic wasn't anywhere close to thinking that. But he wanted to make himself look vulnerable. The kids were more likely to help him, more likely to take it seriously if they thought his friends were in real danger.

"I think it's a possibility. Especially after what happened to your friend."

The three teens stared at him.

"What specifically did happen, if you don't mind my asking?"

Alex cleared his throat and shook his head. "I don't know. Just that it—the gargun was out there, chasing me and Kyle. I tried to fight it off, to save him, you know? But it was too powerful."

"Wait, what?" Katie exclaimed. "I thought you didn't see it?"

"I didn't," Alex quickly said. "It was too dark and I thought it was a man. Someone out there, stalking us. Like a serial killer or something, you know? I just saw Kyle struggling with someone. So, I jumped in, tried to get in a few good punches."

Lydia frowned and glanced away.

Alex rubbed his nose. "But it was strong. It threw me down and I must have, I don't know. Blacked out for a few minutes or something."

"What?" Lydia said. "You didn't tell me that. Did you go to the hospital?"

"Nah. I didn't tell my parents. I…I just freaked. I didn't feel bad afterward, like no headache or anything. So, I just went home. And then we spent some time down at the police station. They called in Deputy Pepper who took forever to get there and then asked a crap ton of questions. I think he wanted to pin it on me or something."

"That's standard procedure," Katie said. "My father worked with Sheriff Rinko for years and it's like the law or something. You have to question any other people on the scene of an accident."

"Yeah. Well, it sucked. I mean, I still couldn't believe he was gone, you know?" Alex glanced around at the faces staring back at him. "Like gone, gone. Never-coming-back gone. It's still weird to think about it."

"I know," Lydia said quietly. "Even after we saw him at the mo—" she stopped suddenly, looked at Vic with wide eyes.

"You went to see your friend at the morgue?" Vic asked.

Lydia glanced at her friends. Katie shook her head slightly, but Lydia took a deep breath and nodded. "Yeah. We were looking for something."

"The gargun's mark," Vic said.

Lydia looked surprised and nodded again. "You heard us by the General Store."

"Guilty."

Katie sighed in exasperation. "Great. Smart, Lydia, really smart. Now the whole town will know." She glared at Vic as though he was already running from the room, yelling the information at the top of his lungs.

He put his hands up to signify innocence. "They won't hear it from me. But can I ask you something?"

He looked at Lydia again. She studied a hangnail intently,

161

rubbed a thumb over it.

"What is the mark? And why did you think your friend had one?"

Lydia glanced up at Vic, her cheeks slightly pink. "In our American History class. We were assigned a topic and had to research it and write a really long essay."

"That sucked," Alex chimed in. Katie remained silent but glared at Lydia.

"My topic was the history of the Salem Witch Trials. Not only here in the US, though I did write about that. But earlier. Back in Europe. One of the things that the people being accused of witchcraft supposedly had was this mark on them, made by the devil. It was a curved line, somewhere on their body, usually their torso. It was supposed to be made by either the devil's talon scratched against the skin, or his tongue burning them. Like a brand, you know?"

Vic nodded.

"Anyway, I thought that maybe, if it really was the gargun that had gotten Kyle, then he might have left a mark. Because of the legend, you know?" She stared at her hangnail. "So, we snuck into the morgue—"

Katie sighed and threw up her hands.

"It was my idea," Alex said.

Lydia continued. "We snuck in to check both the bodies: Kyle's and Sheriff Rinko's."

"And they both had the mark?"

Lydia and Alex exchanged a look and nodded.

Katie put her hands over her face and moaned. "This is so messed up."

"What do you think it means?" Vic asked, wondering if it would be inappropriate to ask them to repeat this story while he filmed.

"I don't know," Alex said. "But maybe it goes back to the pact that guy had with the devil."

"Here we go," Katie said and flopped on the bed.

"Come on, Katie," Alex replied. "If Mr. Mellin's here to investigate the gargun, don't you think he's heard the stories already?"

Vic had no idea what they were talking about but played along.

He nodded. "Sure, but I haven't heard your version. And please, call me Vic. Mr. Mellin makes me feel like an old fart."

Alex grinned and straightened his shoulders, seeming to enjoy the spotlight. But was that because he believed the story he was going to tell or did he just like the limelight? Vic was still trying to wrap his brain around the information that Lydia had shared: devil's marks and witches and the fact that the two bodies here had similar marks on them.

He leaned forward in his chair and Alex started.

"Okay, so there was this guy, Jenson Briggs..."

Chapter 21

Vic Mellin

The next morning, the little group met again, this time outside of Vic's motel. It was Friday and the sun shone hotly against his neck as he loaded video equipment into the van. They were taking a little field trip—him and the three kids—first to one of the cabins that Lydia's mom rented out and then back down to Gargun's Footstool. The kids said that no one would be down there yet. The volunteer fire department set up the fireworks but didn't start until well after lunch. By then, Vic and the kids would be gone.

He hoped.

Showing up at the cabin would be strange and he'd spent a good chunk of time sipping his morning coffee trying to work out a plausible explanation for whoever was staying there.

"Good morning. Mind if we poke around in your yard?" He'd imagined asking the person who opened the door. Maybe he could tell him or her that he was teaching a summer class to the teens on lighting and they'd just happened to be hiking by...it sounded too stupid even before he said it. He'd have to think of something better on the way.

Vic called the front desk, asked if there were any messages

but there weren't. He checked his cell phone. No texts. The little icon was blank though. He hit the button to check for recent calls but that too was empty. A sick feeling rolled around in his belly. What had happened to Nikki and Joe?

A knock sounded on the door of his room, and he went to open it and drained his coffee mug at the same time.

"We're ready if you are," Alex slouched near the door, his tan legs dark against gray sports shorts. Lydia stood beside him looking pale and tired.

"No Katie?" Vic motioned for them to come inside. They did but left the door open. Vic put the cup on the desk and glanced around. He doubted the maid would steal and hawk the leftover tech equipment but shoved it into a bag and pushed it under the bed just in case.

"No, she's gone to her aunt's today with her mom. They're in charge of the parade and there's a bunch of stuff they have to do to get ready for it," Lydia said.

Vic nodded. "All right. Let's go."

They bounced around on dirt roads, Vic following Lydia's verbal instructions until they climbed a steep hill—or maybe it would be considered a small mountain?—tangled with thick brush. In some places, overgrown branches scraped against the sides of the van.

When they pulled into the narrow gravel driveway, they saw two vehicles already parked there. One was a Lexus, the other a beat-up Jeep Cherokee. Vic's heart sank. He'd hoped no one would be there and he could look around without having to give a half-assed explanation.

When the little group stepped out of the van, Vic still hadn't thought of a good reason to ask to poke around. He'd have to rely on the documentary: tell whoever was staying here that he wanted to get some rural footage.

"Hello," a man's voice rang out in the hot morning air. "Can I help you?"

Vic waved and walked over, the kids trailing behind him.

"Victor Mellin," he said. "I'm with Backyard Films and am doing a little—"

"Oh, hey, yeah. I recognize you. I'm Tony Bradford. You were looking for your friends yesterday down at the lake."

Vic vaguely remembered the man sitting next to Jessica Brown.

"Did they show up?" Tony asked.

Vic shook his head. "No, not yet."

"Hmm," Tony made a concerned noise in his throat and glanced from Vic to Alex and Lydia. "Hi guys," he said. "You must be looking for Jessica. She's the one staying here. I was just helping her...uh, look for something."

"Hello," Jessica appeared from the woods bordering the property. She dusted her hands together. They were covered in soil. Strange to be gardening when you were staying at someone else's cabin, Vic thought.

"Good to see you again," she said. "Did you find your friends?" she asked Vic.

Vic shook his head.

"Hi Ms. Brown," Lydia said.

Jessica smiled. "Lydia, right?"

The girl nodded. Vic had forgotten that this was Lydia's family's cabin. He could have saved himself a lot of trouble and just asked her who was staying there.

"What can I help you with?" Jessica's smile stayed firmly in place, but she glanced over her shoulder toward a small clump of pine trees, distracted.

"I'm doing some filming of the area, for the documentary," Vic said. "And was hoping to get a little footage here. Just outside," he rushed on before Jessica could object to opening her home to him and his camera.

"It's one of the oldest properties in the area," Lydia piped up helpfully.

"Oh. I'm sorry but now's not a good time." Again, Jessica glanced over her shoulder. Vic tilted his position slightly, trying to see what it was that she was looking at, or for, but couldn't see anything other than trees. Wait. What was that?

He glanced back at Jessica, but she was listening to Lydia who was telling her that the road the cabin was on was the oldest in the area. He took a single step to the side. Tony caught his eye and raised his brows questioningly. But not before Vic had seen the overturned earth near a small grove of trees.

"Planting some flowers?" he asked when there was a lull in the conversation. He nodded toward the dirt pile.

Jessica flushed. "No, I..." she looked at Lydia apologetically. "I'll get it all put back before your mom sees, I promise."

Lydia laughed. "I doubt Mom would care. As long as you're not, like, stealing endangered plants to take back with you to the city."

"No, I have a brown thumb."

"So, what were you digging up back there?" Vic asked.

Jessica and Tony glanced at each other.

"Well..." Jessica started and then broke off. She was quiet for a few long seconds, thinking. Then, "Look. This needs to be completely off the record." She looked at Vic.

He nodded. "Sure, of course."

"I saw something out here last night." She glanced at Tony. "Or someone, I guess you could say." Her hands shook as she smoothed them over her shorts.

"A stalker?" Lydia asked. "That's crazy. I mean—"

"You mean the gargun, don't you?" Alex interrupted.

Jessica and Tony glanced at each other again and some unasked question was answered.

"Maybe," Jessica said, her voice quiet. "I think maybe it was."

The group was silent for a second. Then Lydia spoke up. "Where?"

Jessica pointed back toward the tightly knit pine trees.

"So, that's why you dug it up?" Lydia asked.

Jessica nodded. "I saw…I saw a light when it was there. It was looking at it. I thought we'd find, I don't know. An old solar light or a broken outdoor lantern or something. But we found a ledger instead. In a metal box."

"Can we see it?" Alex asked and took a step toward the trees.

Jessica looked helplessly at Tony. He shrugged, raised his eyebrows in a look that read, "it's your call."

She bit her lip, then nodded.

"Sure, I guess. But remember, off the record." She stared at Vic.

He nodded. "We found something out too." He glanced from Lydia to Alex and back. "Share and share alike, right?"

Lydia nodded first, then Alex.

"What about?" Tony asked.

"The gargun," Alex said. "And my friend who died." He glanced around at the choking, tangled woods.

The little group walked together to the small mound of dirt. Laid to the side of it was an empty, rusted metal box near a discarded sweatshirt.

"I wrapped it up in this," Jessica said and bent and carefully revealed an old, brown book nestled in the shirt.

She held the book flat in her hands and opened the cover. Vic could smell the mustiness when he squatted next to her. The pages were yellowed and faded but they were right, it was a ledger of some sort. There were columns, some with numbers others with initials. The first entry stated, "#1: H.B", and on the second line, "#2: BG". On the line below that "#3: EK," was recorded. Along each of these columns was another with a list of eight-digit numbers.

"Are those years?" Tony asked, pointing.

"I think so," Jessica said.

"So, you've got what, three initials for the first date, in 1820," Lydia said, pointing a finger at the column. "And then it's," she paused her lips moving slightly. "1845 before the next entries. And there's six of those."

"Yeah, and there's nine in the next entry."

"What's the year for those?" Vic asked. It was hard to see from the angle where he was.

"Uh, 1870."

"Anyone good at math?" Tony asked. No one responded. All eyes were on the book in Jessica's hands.

"In 1895 there were," Alex paused. "Eleven."

"Oh, I was thinking it had to do with primary numbers," Jessica said.

"There's got to be a pattern here, with the number of initials per date," Vic said, taking a step closer. "And what are all of these?" He pointed to the column of initials. "People?"

"We think so," Tony said.

"People that the gargun…killed?" Lydia's voice was a near whisper.

Jessica and Tony glanced at each other.

"We're not sure," Tony said. "It's just that if you look at the end of the entries," he flipped forward in the book. The ink there was darker, more recently added to the page, Vic realized. "Check out these initials," Tony pointed.

"R.R. and K.L. K.L., as in Kyle Lanphere?" Alex asked.

Lydia put a hand over her mouth, a small, anguished sound escaped from between her fingers.

"It could be but we don't know anything for sure," Jessica said.

"Wow, this is really sick," Lydia said, her voice a pinched whisper. "Then the R.R. is Sheriff Rinko."

"What was his first name?" Tony asked.

"Robert."

There was more silence, broken only by the whine of cicadas already gearing up for the heat of the day.

"So, let's go back to the dates and the number of people," Vic said. "The dates are twenty-five years apart. But what about the initials? It could just be a coincidence, that there isn't a pattern as far as those go."

"Yeah, but look," Alex said, tracing his finger over the ledger's columns. "They repeat themselves. See? After eleven, it goes to thirteen. But the next batch starts over again at three. Then six is the entry after that. By the time you get here—" he pointed at the date of 1995. "It's up to nine again."

"And this year is the twenty-fifth one," Lydia sounded excited. "So that means that this year it will be eleven again."

"Eleven people killed." Jessica's voice was soft and disbelieving.

"The gargun is supposed to appear every twenty-five years, right? But why? And why those numbers?" Lydia asked.

A bead of sweat trickled between Vic's shoulders.

The group was silent for several long minutes, each one trying to work out the math. "I think I know," Tony said finally. "In occultism, those are considered special numbers. Three, six, nine, eleven, and thirteen. And then multiples of them too, like thirty-three, seventy-seven."

"Should we be worried about why you know this?" Jessica tried to laugh but it sounded more like she was choking.

"It was a class I took during seminary."

"So, those are all bad numbers?" Lydia asked.

Tony nodded. "If you're not an occult member, then yes. And triplicate numbers are even worse. Or better, depending which side of the fence you're on."

"What's a triplicate number?" Jessica asked.

"It's just a fancy way of saying numbers in sequence that are identical: like one-hundred eleven, three-hundred thirty-three, and so on."

Not the right time to ask, but Vic wondered if Tony would be willing to appear on video with this information sometime soon. It would help add credibility to both the ledger and the story of the gargun to have a man of the cloth spout the hypothesis, rather than just a couple of kids or even Jessica. Though she would look great on camera. Part of his brain was already mapping out the shot, imagining the questions he'd ask.

"What if you added up all the initials so far?" Jessica asked. "Anyone have a calculator handy?"

Vic pulled out his nearly useless cell phone. "Someone read me the numbers."

Jessica did and Vic tapped them into the screen.

"It comes up to sixty if you don't count the sheriff and the boy that died."

"Kyle," Alex said. "His name was Kyle."

"Sorry," Vic mumbled.

"And if this year's number is eleven, then it would be—" Jessica said.

"Seventy-seven." Lydia interrupted; her eyes wide.

"That's not good," Tony said. "Not only is it a double number but seven is considered the universal sacred number."

"Really? I thought it was just lucky when you were playing roulette?" Vic joked but no one laughed.

"That's the reason that many people consider it lucky. Because it's supposed to be a number tied into spirituality."

"Well," Jessica closed the book. "We've got a lot of theories, but we don't know anything for sure. We've got to find answers. If the ledger is true and eleven people are going to die in 2020, then we need to do something to stop it."

"Not only eleven in 2020," Tony said. "Legend says that the gargun only comes back for six days. You first saw him three nights ago. That was the first of the six. Which means he has three nights left. And nine more people to kill."

Vic felt a pasty film in his throat and tried to swallow it down.

"Seven." His voice croaked. "Seven if it got Nikki and Joe."

Chapter 22

Penny Donovan

"Y ou too, Mrs. Mills. We'll see you at the festival!" Penny said with a friendly wave. Mrs. Mills, the last check-in for the weekend had finally arrived with her family. Her husband—tired after the long drive, Mrs. Mills had said, had huffed and puffed impatiently by their luxury SUV while Penny had checked the family in. Two kids—both whining about the lack of Wi-Fi and picking up then nearly dropping everything that wasn't nailed down, had driven Penny nearly mad in the ten minutes they'd been in the reception area. But she'd kept a smile on her face and loosened the grip on her pen before it snapped in two.

Before the Mills family had arrived, Penny had been answering hiking questions for the Vanders—now those were people who seemed poorly matched, she thought as she tucked files back into the cabinet and straightened her desk. Rubin Vander was as passive as his wife, Barbara, was aggressive. And neither of them seemed like outdoorsy types. As though sensing Penny's opinion, Barbara had given a highlight reel of some of their greatest adventures while traveling the world. Penny shook her head and tossed two stray paperclips into the little ceramic dish

Lydia had made in second grade. Now that the guests were all settled, or on their way to being so, she'd better start painting the trim. It was a job Lydia was supposed to do today.

Where was Lydia? Penny wondered again. She'd left a granola bar wrapper on the counter along with a half-finished glass of juice from breakfast. Penny glanced at her watch. It was only half-past nine but already the heat made her shirt cling uncomfortably to her back. She pinched the polo shirt stamped with the Cedar Grove Properties logo and fanned it a few times.

She'd better not be at the pool, Penny thought with irritation as she gathered the paint and brush and a little broom to get rid of any clinging cobwebs. And Lydia could forget about going unchaperoned to the opening ceremony tonight if this was how she was going to act. But a twinge of worry spasmed in Penny's belly. It wasn't like Lydia. She always left a note if she was going out to run an errand.

Twenty-five hot minutes later, Penny heard gravel crunching underfoot and glanced behind her. Clare Snelling jogged up the driveway. Penny smiled, used to seeing Clare run along the road almost daily, no matter the weather.

"Did you hear?" Clare slowed down to a walk and put her hands on her hips. Her face glistened with sweat and the little belt of pink-capped bottles she wore around her waist were half-empty.

"Hear what?" Penny set her paint brush down and arched her back to relieve the strain there.

"About the…bodies."

Penny stared at her blankly.

"They just found two bodies on the marshy side of the lake, a man and a woman. A fisherman was out with his grandson and caught a body instead." Clare grimaced. Penny felt her stomach dip.

"Oh my God."

"I know. It's hard to believe, isn't it? And so close to the festival too," Clare shook her head sorrowfully. "I shouldn't be thinking about that now of course, but it's certainly poor timing. Jim is sure to see a drop off in sales when the news gets out."

Clare's husband, Jim, ran what amounted to fishing and scenic boat tours of the area, though Clare labeled them, "adventure tours". She was also quick to point out to potential customers that Jim's family could trace their lines back several generations in the area.

"No one knows the hidden mysteries of this landscape better than Jim," she'd say with a perky smile. "But you can get a hearty taste, for only $79.99."

"That's awful." Penny's thoughts immediately went to her missing daughter. Oh, God. What if—

"The bodies weren't recognized, or I should say, recognizable," Clare answered Penny's unasked question and wrinkled her nose, then pulled out one of the little bottles of water and drank deeply.

"How do you mean?" Penny hesitated. "Recognizable?"

"Well, they'd been in the water for a little while." Clare shivered and capped the bottle. "And they were tourists, at least that's what I heard. City dressed; you know?"

Penny nodded dumbly. She felt a mix of shame over her relief and sadness in equal measure.

"I hope it wasn't any of my guests." Penny mentally reviewed her cabins and their occupants. "Probably not. I didn't have any couples this time. Two singles and the rest families. Still..." her voice drifted off.

Clare nodded. "And on opening day, too."

"What will they do?" Penny asked. "About the festival. Will it be canceled?"

"Not sure," Clare adjusted the sun visor, tucking loose strands of damp hair back into place. "The deputy and mayor and some concerned business owners are meeting at noon. That's why I stopped by. I thought you might want to attend."

"I will. Thanks for letting me know about it."

"The officials want to meet before the state people come in. You know, the murder squad." Clare gave a theatrical shiver.

"Murder squad?" Penny's stomach dipped again. "But these were accidents."

"Well, the first two were, but I guess things look fishy about the tourists. I heard," Clare lowered her voice. "That one of them was decapitated."

Penny's knees wobbled and she put a hand on the nearby lamppost. "What?"

Clare pressed her lips together and nodded. "Anyway, I'm not sure when the state detectives will get here or what they'll tell us when they do as far as the lake is concerned." She glanced at her large fitness watch. "I've got to finish my run before Jim heads out with his first group of the day."

Penny's eyes widened.

"He's taking them trout fishing up at one of the creeks, don't worry," Clare said. "I need to man the shop. We've got a lot of boat rentals lined up for the fireworks tonight. Lots of families were planning afternoon picnics and fishing too, but now I seriously doubt anyone will want to go out on the lake, even if they can." Clare's mouth pulled down at the corners. "If we can keep it quiet though, just for the weekend..."

Penny nodded. While she felt terrible for the accident victims, not being able to use the lake would be a serious problem for her business and a lot of others in town too. Their livelihoods depended on Stillwater Lake, at this time of the year more than any other.

"Thanks for stopping by and letting me know about... everything."

"Sure thing. See you at the meeting."

Penny waved absently as Clare jogged back down the short drive and out onto the street.

Two people dead. Another accident. There had been a little squall yesterday afternoon. Maybe their boat had capsized, or they'd lost control of a canoe or kayaks. She hadn't thought to ask Clare if the two had rented one of Jim's boats, though she was pretty sure Clare wouldn't have told her the truth even if he had. It would be bad for business and Clare was shrewd.

Penny put away her brushes and paint and left a note on the office door, letting anyone who stopped by know that she'd be back by two. Then she hurriedly showered. The hot water felt wonderful on her back, but even as the suds ran down Penny couldn't stop thinking of the two people who'd died. Or of Clare's ominous words: "...one of them had been decapitated."

**

"This is not an ideal situation, no matter how you look at it." The mayor, jowly cheeks flushed said, and leaned on the table at the front of the conference room. It must have been ninety degrees, but Penny had given up waving the tepid air with her checkbook and instead, ran a finger over her hairline every once in a while, wiping away the sweat.

"But the truth of the matter is," Mayor Bloomberg said, over the murmur growing louder in the room. "That four people have died in and around the lake in the past few days. Now, none of us want to appear cold-hearted or unfeeling to the victims' families." He glanced around the room, his gaze fixing on Mrs. Morehouse, one of the loudest voices protesting that the festival go on as planned.

"And while we convey our deepest sympathy to those grieving, we also know the essential nature of the festival on the community at large. Canceling now would not only cause hardship for local shops and restaurants this year but also in the future. Disappointed, even angry guests, leaving our town will talk. They'll tell their friends and family and then, well—" the mayor broke off. His hands rose in a helpless gesture.

"And then we'll all be in trouble, that's what." Penny turned to the woman sitting three seats down. It was Marnie Lareau who owned the only flower shop in town. Stillwater was small, but there were always weddings and funerals and birthdays to be celebrated no matter the capita. Plus, the Gargun Festival Committee hired her annually to put together the fresh urns of flowers that lined Main Street.

"I call for a vote," Marnie continued. When Mrs. Morehouse put a finger in the air and started to counter the suggestion, Mayor Bloomberg jumped in.

"A good idea, Marnie. Let's put it to all of you, shall we?"

He nodded to his secretary who looked as hot and frazzled as everyone else in the room. She handed out slips of paper at the end of each row which were quickly passed down. A random collection of pens and pencils followed.

They'd been in the meeting for more than an hour and a half and Penny was anxious to get out of the stuffy, enclosed space and on with the mountain of work that waited for her back at the office. She knew how she'd be voting and suspected she was in the majority.

Ten minutes later the slips had been collected and counted at the big front table while the crowd murmured and mumbled, each sharing his or her reasons why the festival should or shouldn't go on.

"If I could have your attention, please." The mayor's voice rang through the room and the loud buzz of voices died down.

"The decision has been made to hold this weekend's gargun festival as planned. The sheriff's office and I will be working with state officials when they arrive to see about logistics. At least part of the lake will likely be off-limits. Worst case scenario, we'll have to move tonight's festivities up to Main Street and forgo the fireworks. But hopefully, that won't be the case.

"Folks," he looked around the room, his hangdog face looked more tired than usual. "Even if you weren't on the winning end of this vote, I ask that you do your best to make the festival a success. I don't need to tell any of you how important it is to Stillwater. Not only to those of us in this room but to our children and their futures."

Penny had anticipated a few snarky remarks under the breath of those who'd voted to cancel, but the room was silent except for the lethargic fan blades that moved the air ineffectively.

"Now," he waved a hand. "We'll post a notice at the general store as soon as we know more about those logistics I mentioned, as well as outside this office. Thank you all, for your commitment to your community."

The murmur of the crowd turned louder once again as people moved toward the door in an uneven single file line. Penny started to feel lightheaded and left as soon as she could get to a door. A mix of emotions followed her outside into the relatively cool air: relief the strongest.

Chapter 23

Barbara Vander
The Base of Elmer's Point Trail

"Almost ready?" Rubin called.

Barbara rolled her eyes. "I'll be back shortly. I need to use the facilities."

Rubin sighed. "I've had time to pack up the entire camp. What have you been doing?"

"Painting my nails," Barbara said bitterly. "Idiot." She muttered under her breath.

"We need to leave in ten."

Barbara didn't bother answering. She walked deeper into the woods, intent on finding a spot to relieve herself. What a waste this trip had been, a mistake from the start. The only positive thing about it was that they'd be able to tell a good war story about climbing Elmer's Point, one of the most inhospitable mountains in New England. It was the sole reason Barbara had agreed to come on this trip in the first place. Spending time alone with Rubin in the middle of nowhere wasn't her idea of a good time.

It was hard to believe she and Rubin had ever been good together. That old saying, "absence makes the heart grow fonder" hadn't ever been true for them. Rubin's work required a lot of out-of-town meetings. Some months, Barbara felt more like a single woman than a wife. Maybe if they'd had kids, Barbara thought but instantly pushed the idea away. If they'd had kids, it would have been even worse. Then, instead of working on her committees and having a life of her own, she'd have been forced to lug around whining brats, wiping noses, and constantly handing out snacks like a human vending machine. She'd watched her friends over the years change into shadows of their former selves. It was as though their children sucked the life out of them, leaving them apologetic, overweight, and unkempt versions of the women she used to know. And forget about asking them to go out for drinks, to the spa, or on weekend trips. Weekends, it turned out, were for shuttling children from home to field, as her friends juggled baseball, soccer, lacrosse, and other sports depending on the season.

No thank you. Barbara grimaced as she found a bush to squat behind. In that one area at least, she and Rubin had always seen eye to eye. They'd adventured all over the world together. It was the one thing they enjoyed doing together. Though in recent years they'd pretty much ignored each other once they'd reached their destination.

She took out the little bunch of toilet paper and used it. In the woods, one was supposed to dig a cat hole and bury it or carry the soiled paper back out in a bag for future disposal. But Barbara was tired. She simply wanted to get back to town and put some distance—literal distance—between herself and Rubin. If she had to listen to him whining one more time about his aching back—

A branch snapped nearby. Barbara zipped up her Arc'teryx shorts and turned toward the sound. Probably a squirrel.

They'd seen a lot of them on this hike, more than other places in New England they'd hiked—

Barbara stopped, sensing something wasn't right. What was that? She peered into the shadowy undergrowth and tangle of tree branches behind her. There was something there—some sort of figure. It moved in the shadows. The trees were so close together that they created a natural privacy screen. Barbara squinted, moved a couple of steps closer. The lower tree branches dipped so low to the earth that Barbara couldn't even make out the trunks.

She was sure she'd seen something. And it hadn't been tree trunks.

She took a couple more steps and listened.

Nothing.

Barbara scanned the area again but couldn't see anything. Her imagination had been playing tricks. Giving a half-hearted chuckle, she dusted her hands on her shorts and started back to camp.

They'd stumbled in late last night after having gotten misplaced on the descending trail. Rubin had insisted that he knew where they were. The fact that he didn't and hadn't let on for more than an hour had kept them in the woods a night longer than they'd intended. When he'd looked at the map this morning, he'd realized his error and the fact that they were close to the base of the trail. Idiot was too benign a word to describe Rubin, Barbara thought. With a grim smile, she retraced her steps back to camp.

Suddenly, a flurry of movement came from the trees behind her. Barbara whirled; her eyes wide. There was no hesitation now, no wondering if what she'd seen was just a shadow.

A dark, bulky figure emerged from the boughs. It was half

bent over and wore a black, tattered cape. Barbara was frozen, unable to blink or breathe.

The creature ran toward her. She was so frightened she couldn't even scream. Its gray, pallid face was close to hers. It made a horrible sound as its hands bit into the flesh around her neck. Barbara gasped—or tried to. She couldn't breathe. Couldn't move. Around her the forest was full of noises: birds chattering, animals going about their daily routines and further away, Rubin cursing as he loaded up the pack.

Barbara stared in frozen terror at the darkly lined face that filled her vision. White eyes—bulging and without a pupil or iris stared into her own. The edges of her vision were becoming as gray as the thing's face. She choked, gasped, tried to scream.

This can't be happening, she thought. She wanted to tell it—the thing that held her in its grip that this wasn't real, not possible. But all that came from her throat was a disgusting-sounding gurgle.

***

Rubin sighed and swiped a hand over his forehead. It wasn't even noon yet and already he was damp with sweat. He took a swig from his filtered water bottle and grimaced at the warmth. He was ready for a shower and a nap, followed by a scotch and cigar on the lawn of the inn where they were staying. Now that he had camp packed up, he was impatient to get moving.

Where was Barbara? It shouldn't take that long to pee. He double-checked that the fire was completely out and that the pack was fully battened. He couldn't believe how much stuff two people required for a simple overnight or two in the woods. What would their ancestors think of the cushy way they camped in this century? Rubin could imagine his great-grandmother shaking her head in disgust.

"In my day, we didn't have such comforts," she would have said, in her thick German accent. "What a pampered man you turned into, Rubin."

True, but I've worked hard to get where I am he argued back with *Uroma*. His great-grandmother had never approved of Barbara. "She is *emporkömmling*," Uroma had said more than once, lifting her nose in the air and mimicking Barbara sauntering with her head held high. *Emporkömmling*, a snob or social climber.

Barbara simply had good taste; he'd joked with his family. After all, she'd chosen Rubin, hadn't she? It had been the couple's shared love of travel that entwined them early on. Together they'd parasailed off the Greek islands, cruised down the Nile River, and gone on wild game hunts in Australia and Africa. They'd seen the Great Wall of China and the pyramids stayed in a small cottage in Cotswolds and visited Mayan ruins in South America. Of course, the trips to exotic locations had fizzled with time. As had their marriage. But Rubin worked nearly eighty hours a week and Barbara was always busy with her volunteering and clubs and God knew what else. It was rare to spend much time together. They still traveled as a couple. Only now it was semi-annual trips, and they usually did their own thing once arriving at their destination.

But he'd thought, he'd hoped, that this trip would be a nice way to reconnect. He'd pictured them enjoying long glasses of wine after dinner, walking hand-in-hand through the town's rustic streets, and hiking in the mountains, enjoying morning coffee by a babbling brook. Only, it hadn't worked out that way. Instead of helping them fall back in love, it seemed the more time the couple spent together, the more they noticed how much they disliked each other.

"Barbara," Rubin called, imagining his wife rolling her eyes and mumbling under her breath. "Everything okay?"

No response.

Rubin checked the site one last time and headed toward the place where Barbara had disappeared. She would be irritated with him, no doubt, for checking up on her. But what if she'd fallen? The trails around her were not especially well marked and there were often steep drop-offs with no warnings on the mountains.

The forest was dense. Rubin pushed through tangled vines and thick pine branches. Ahead and to the right, there was a sound.

"Barbara?"

The sun was momentarily blotted out by clouds and the entire forest was suddenly devoid of color. It was strange like a color movie had suddenly turned black and white. A mosquito whined near Rubin's ear. He felt something touch his ankle and shook it off without looking.

"Barbara?" he called again. A light breeze whistling through the upper branches of the trees was all he heard. Rubin stepped forward—or tried to—when the thing around his ankle bit into it.

He glanced down. Something was around it, twisted and metallic. A wire? But that didn't make sense. He must have stepped into a trap, a snare, he thought. Would they allow hunting in a hiking area though? Surely there would have been signs if—

Ahead of Rubin the thick branches parted. At first, he couldn't see anything other than the gentle sway of the tree's lower branches. He expected to see Barbara step from the darkness, her face a thundercloud.

Instead, another figure stood in the now-empty space. It was dark and hunched with a strange gray face that looked toward Rubin. It wore a mask of some sort with bulging white eyes.

"Hey! What the hell do you think you're doing?" Rubin yelled still struggling to free his ankle.

"Barbara!" he called. The thing moved toward him surprisingly graceful. Rubin kicked and jerked against the wire but doing so only made it tighter. He felt something warm dripping into his sock and knew without looking that it was blood.

The masked form drew closer. What was this? Rubin thought. His mind was filled with images of movies about serial killers he'd watched as a teen. Was this Stillwater's version of Michael Myers or Jason Vorhees? Some weird, backwoods yokel's idea of a joke?

Rubin was panting and felt a rise of shame in his belly. His hands instinctively went into fists though. As soon as the dark-robed thing came within range, Rubin shot them out in quick succession: *one-two-three. Jab, jab, jab.*

But the other man stepped back easily. Rubin did the same, trying to put more distance between himself and the robed man that stood in front of him. Unexpectedly, it grimaced and lunged toward Rubin. Something silver shone in its hand, its talons. Rubin realized seconds before the dagger plunged into his chest. He stared in horror unable to make a sound. He saw the knife but couldn't believe it was real. Then fiery liquid pain tore through his chest.

Breathing raggedly, Rubin put a hand over the dagger. The handle was warm. He looked from it back to the creature. The man-thing moved toward him again and put its claw-like hand over Rubin's. Falling backward, Rubin felt a burning arc of pain in his ankle. But his chest—he looked again—his chest felt like molten lava was being poured into it. A few steady trickles of blood meandered from the hilt of the knife.

Rubin saw the creature standing above him now. Its eyes were all wrong, Rubin thought.

And then everything faded to black.

Chapter 24

Jessica Brown

"Believe me, I know how crazy this sounds," Jessica said, putting her hands on the edge of the sheriff's desk. "And I wouldn't be coming to you if I wasn't sure that people here in Stillwater are in danger. There are four people dead now. Four—"

"Yes, ma'am, I'm aware of that. Four fatal accidents in our small town are a lot to deal with. Which is why I need to get back to my work. Now, if you'll excuse me—"

"Accidents? Are you sure they were accidents? I think that these were planned," Jessica lowered her voice. "Murders. And what happens if more people die on your watch?" Jessica interrupted the deputy's attempt to usher her out of the room with a hand on the doorframe. "Do you want that on your conscience?"

"Ma'am, you can rest assured that we're doing everything possible to keep the people of Stillwater safe. Now, I'm mighty busy. The officials have this well in hand. Now if you'll—"

"I can't believe this," Jessica threw up her hands.

"Believe it," Deputy Pepper said and holding her arm firmly, guided Jessica from the hot office.

After depositing her on the sidewalk outside the building and wishing her a good day, the deputy retreated up the stairs and closed the door firmly behind him. Jessica looked around. The sidewalks were mobbed with people, most walking around and pointing out landmarks, some with dripping ice cream cones or paper cups of slushies from the general store, others consulting maps and snapping pictures of Main Street.

It was beautiful, Jessica thought. The parade committee had wound garlands of paper flowers over each of the wrought iron lampposts and strung more of these, along with festive purple lights between each post. A canopy of lights and flowers was mixed with tiny, brightly-colored pennants tucked into large pots overflowing with geraniums, petunias, and some other white cascading flowers Jessica didn't recognize. If you didn't know what was going on, it would be like any other fun, lighthearted day in smalltown America, Jessica thought.

She pulled her floppy hat back onto her head and plunged into the crowd. If they couldn't get help from the authorities, then Jessica, Tony, and the others would have to take matters into their own hands. Unfortunately, they hadn't figured out a way to do that yet.

Only Tony waited for her in the little park outside of Vic's motel.

"How's he doing?" Jessica asked, nodding toward Vic's room. After learning about his two crew members' deaths, he'd retreated into the room. That had been more than two hours ago.

"Not sure," Tony responded. He sat backward on one side of the picnic table. "I knocked once, asked if there was anything I could do, but he didn't answer the door. How'd it go at the sheriff's?"

190

"Badly."

Tony nodded.

"Where are the kids?"

"Lydia had to go help her mother and Alex went home to check something on his laptop. He said that he had an idea, about the gargun." Tony shrugged.

"We need a plan," Jessica ran her fingers through her hair. "If the deputy isn't going to help us—"

"Guys!" A male voice rang out through the quiet little garden.

Jessica and Tony turned. Alex ran toward them.

"You guys have gotta see this," Alex's voice was excited. "I think it could be important."

The door to Vic's motel room opened and he poked his head out. His eyes were rimmed with pink. He'd aged ten years in the past hour, Jessica thought.

"Vic," Jessica said softly and approached the door. "I'm so sorry about your friends."

"I just got off the phone with their parents. They're… distraught."

"I can imagine," Tony said. "If there's anything I can do—"

"Thanks," Vic said. "But I think for now getting my mind off this will help the most."

Alex interrupted. "You're going to want to see this," he repeated.

Vic shuffled out of the motel room and a sour smell followed him, like the remnants of whiskey or bourbon. She didn't blame him. She'd need a stiff drink or four if she'd had to make the call he had.

"Remember we were talking about those dates and initials?" Alex asked. Jessica struggled to get her mind to switch gears.

"Well, I dug around in the database at the town office and

191

found something interesting."

"You have access to the town's database?" Tony asked.

"Nah. Well, sort of. Katie knows her dad's password and I kind of talked her into giving it to me once, so technically I borrowed his login."

"Great," Tony said. "Now we're encouraging delinquency in the local youth."

Alex grinned briefly. "Look," he said, brandishing a piece of paper.

"What is it?" Jessica asked.

All three adults bent their heads over the page. It was a printout showing dates—the same dates from the ledger, Jessica realized. Alongside it was another list of numbers.

"We were right," Alex said. "See?" He stabbed at the numbers in the second and third column with a finger. "Those are the years of birth," he said, pointing to the first one. "And those are the deaths." He moved his finger over to the second. "They match up to real people in town. I didn't have time to check the whole list, but I did a sample—like five or so. And they match."

A buzz of excitement filled Jessica's chest like a little swarm of bees.

"So, it's true." Vic breathed. "Those initials were all deaths recorded."

"Yeah," Alex agreed.

"It confirms what we thought," Tony said. "But I'm not sure it will convince the deputy or anyone else in charge."

"Yeah, good luck with that," Jessica took her hat off and swept her hair into a twist. Her neck was already damp from the heat.

"We don't need to," Alex said. "We just need to figure out where and when the gargun might strike again and prevent it."

"Okay. And how are we going to do that?" Tony asked. He

looked at Alex seriously. Jessica liked how Tony treated the teens like people, not patronizing them the way lots of adults did—rolling their eyes and making sarcastic jokes about them or their opinions.

"There must be a pattern," Alex said.

"Yeah, good idea. Patterns are important. What do we know about the gargun and his tactics?" Tony adjusted his ball cap.

"He likes to get people alone," Jessica said. "Or at least without an audience."

"The deaths have all happened down at the lake or near it," Alex added.

"Good, that's good," Tony said. "What else?"

"They've all happened in the late afternoon or evening," Vic added. "Well, as far as we know."

"Okay," Tony said. "Hang on a second…" he pulled the oilskin ledger free from his pocket and ran his fingers over the pages. "Let's look at this again. If the dates line up—"

A loose, yellowed paper fluttered from the pages and fell to the ground. Alex reached down and picked it up, then unfolded it.

"Woah," Alex said. "It's really old."

They all watched as Alex read silently for a few seconds.

"What's it say?" Jessica asked.

Alex handed it to Tony who was standing closest.

Tony cleared his throat and read it aloud. Jessica leaned closer, reading over his shoulder.

I am filled with regret over what I have done. And yet, it is part of my birthright. No blame then should fall on me. But I fear it will in the end.

For the past many centuries, this task has been ours to bear. I wonder if our forefather, Jenson Briggs, could have foreseen the pain and anguish he had projected onto his kin? Surely not, or he would have chosen differently all those years ago.

The ink was smeared a little, making a few words illegible. Then it started a new paragraph.

The birthright of one man's family has destroyed so many others. I am tired to my very bones. The thought of the death and mayhem by my hand...

Again, the ink was smeared. The next line began with the same shaky script.

If only there were a way to break this oath, this contract! If I were a religious man, I would throw myself on the altar and beg for God's mercy on my soul. But I do not believe in fairytales or mythical gods so that I may sleep better at night.

My fate, my future, is my own.

And so, I take this night to cleanse myself from the impurities, from the guilt that weighs on my heart so heavily. I am bound to my fate, my past, my future. It is my burden. Mine alone, to bear.

The letter was signed by Caleb Coventry.

"Wow," Tony said. Then, "Thank God. Now we have a starting point. Or at least another puzzle piece."

Jessica glanced from him to Vic and Alex and back again.

Tony looked worried; his forehead wrinkled. "Jenson Briggs. They were talking about him at the meeting at the historical society."

"Yeah him and some other old fart started this town," Alex

said.

"I don't get what he's talking about. I mean—what's Caleb saying?" Jessica asked. "Somehow humans tie in with the killings the gargun does?"

There was silence for a few long seconds.

"Have you ever seen that ancient movie, *Poltergeist*?" Alex asked. "It must be like that. Like the gargun must overtake them somehow."

"Or maybe there is no gargun," Tony said softly. "Maybe it's just a legend, like so many people think."

"What?" Vic's voice was louder and surer than it had been earlier. "What about the footage I got? You've seen it," he motioned to Alex who nodded vigorously. "If there's no gargun, then what the hell was that...that thing?"

"I don't doubt you saw something, Vic. But we've been quick to assume—and given the circumstances who could blame us—that the gargun was real. A given. But what if there is someone here in town that is covering up their murders by pinning them on the gargun? What did we really see, after all?" Tony asked.

"What I saw was real," Jessica said. "I saw the gargun outside of my cabin."

"Could it have been someone dressed in a costume?" Tony asked. Jessica was about to shoot that idea down but what had she seen? The creature hadn't been floating through the air or shooting lightning bolts out of its hands after all.

"I saw it too," Alex said. "Kyle and me, we both saw it."

"What about the video?" Vic sounded impatient. "How do you explain that?"

"I haven't seen it yet. And I don't," Tony said. "I'm not trying to discount anything any of you have seen. But what if there was another explanation? What if because the gargun is what we've been looking for, been afraid to find, we're seeing it everywhere we go?"

"So, you think it's a person?" Vic's voice was incredulous. "Someone dressed up in a Halloween costume?"

"You mean like a serial killer?" Jessica's voice sounded shaky, and she cleared her throat.

Tony nodded. "Maybe. Look, I'm not saying this letter about Briggs or the gargun isn't true. If anything, this only makes it more valid. But instead of a creature—a monster—going around killing people, maybe it's a person. A resident of Stillwater. Maybe even someone who feels like they need to do their family duty by wiping out some of their neighbors?"

Vic exhaled loudly.

Alex shook his head. "No way, man. There's no way that whatever that thing was we saw that night was a regular person. It had like, ninja skills. You've seen those cliffs! There's no way that someone could have scaled them so easily and snagged Kyle like it did."

"And in the footage—the gargun was sort of, well, hovering is the best word I can use to describe it," Vic said. "It seemed like it was floating there."

"Maybe I'm wrong," Tony said. "But we owe it to everyone in this town to check out all the theories, right? We need to at least consider it, do some research. Maybe there's another reason that the gargun and this," he motioned to the letter. "Caleb Coventry are related."

"We don't have time for research!" Vic rubbed his hands roughly over his face. They rasped over his stubbled cheeks. "People are dying here. Nikki and Joe. The sheriff. The kid, uh, Kyle. Other people are in danger right now. The festival is starting. It's the perfect opportunity for the gargun to pick off more people. He still needs, what, seven?"

"So far he hasn't wanted an audience," Tony said. "Maybe the fact that the kick-off party is happening tonight will work in our favor. Maybe he's going to wait until he can get someone alone."

"Like me at my cabin," Jessica couldn't stop the sudden shiver.

Alex looked nervously over his shoulder, as though expecting the gargun to pop out of a nearby stand of trees any moment.

"We need to split up," Tony said. "A couple of us should go check out Caleb Coventry at the historical society or library. Look up his line of descendants."

"If we traced that line forward," Jessica nodded, "then we'd find out who still lives in the area. It would narrow the pool of potential killers." She couldn't believe she was saying this, that any of this was real.

"Exactly," said Tony. "The other two should head down to the lake. Walk around the crowds on the outskirts and keep an eye out for the gargun…or someone dressed up like him. It would be hard to blend in, so odds are he wouldn't chance it. But if so—"

"I'm on it," Alex said. "I'll grab my old man's pistol and—"

"No way," Tony said. "No guns. Don't you have mace or something?"

"My mom's got that," Alex said. "And maybe I could grab a kitchen knife…"

Tony sighed but Jessica didn't blame Alex. She wished she still had that knife she'd grabbed from the cabin right now.

"Alex can come with me," Vic said. "I might as well get more festival footage anyway. How are you with a camera?"

"Good. I mean, great. I'm on the tech team at my high school and—"

"Perfect. You're my newest employee."

"We'll go to the historical society then," Jessica said. "If they're even open." She glanced at her watch. "If not, we can check out the library and see what town records they have."

Tony frowned. "Without cell phone coverage, it'll be hard for us to stay in touch."

"Oh, I almost forgot. I brought these," Alex handed out two expensive-looking walkie-talkies. "They're mine. I mean when I was a kid. My friend and I used them, and we were across town from each other—they get good range."

"Thanks," Jessica took one of the gray walkie-talkies.

Setting both units on the same channel, they did a quick check to make sure they were working. Then Vic and Alex climbed into the van to go to the lake and Jessica and Tony drove toward Main Street.

Jessica's heart thumped hard in her chest and her hands were damp on the steering wheel. They had to find something. And do it fast.

Chapter 25

Alex Richards

Vic didn't talk much on the way down to the lake, which was fine with Alex. He hated making small talk even though he was pretty good at it. His mother's friends were always commenting about what a nice boy he was, "And so social!" Not like their own kids, they'd grouse, who communicated mostly in grunts. The trick, Alex had learned, was to ask questions. People loved talking about themselves. Then just smiling and nodding most of the time kept them happy and thinking you cared what they were telling you.

The road ahead of the van was lined with cars, trucks, and SUVs. People had parked along the road before it narrowed. At the bottleneck, signs that said, "no parking past this point" were posted and orange tape was strewn over barricades. A large meadow just before it had been turned into a makeshift parking lot. The van jounced over the ruts and Vic found one of the few spots left, in the row furthest away from the throng.

"We should split up," he said and slid the van door open. "But let's keep in range so we can contact the others if we need to." He grabbed a small, black backpack and stuffed a camera, a tripod, and a few other pieces of equipment in.

Alex didn't get what Vic said but nodded anyway.

"Ready?" Vic asked.

Alex nodded. He'd found a hunting knife that had its own little sheath and strapped that to his belt but had skipped the pepper spray. It felt too girlish.

The crowd of festival-goers was thick. Talking, laughing voices filled the air. It was a perfect day for it, Kyle thought. The sun was hot, but a nice breeze flitted off the lake. Puffy, white clouds were strewn across the bright blue sky like lengths of cotton batting. The sight and sounds brought Alex back to childhood: perched on his dad's shoulders, running circles around the quilt his mother had spread for their picnic dinner, the magic of the fireworks and bare feet dipping into the cold lake water.

Now though, he felt as tight and taut as a rubber band. Every loud noise startled him. He scanned the faces in the crowd not for friends and family but the sight of a hooded figure in a dark, tattered robe. He looked at the tree line, sure he was going to see the shadowy figure or the awful white eyes staring back at him.

"Keep your eyes peeled," Vic said. He scanned the crowds too, eyes hidden behind a pair of mirrored sunglasses.

What did he think Alex had been doing? Keeping them closed?

"Look, Mommy!" A little girl's voice rang out, "It's the gargun!"

Alex whirled around, following the girl's pointing finger. A group of college kids had a huge poster of the gargun, one Alex recognized from the general store. They'd mounted it on foam board and a stick and waved it above the crowd as they walked, like a flag. They'd given it an eyepatch and written "Arrg'un,

200

matie!" in big block letters. Streamers floated behind it like ribbons.

"Let's check the cliffs when we get down there," Vic said, and Alex nodded. "What's the schedule like tonight? I forgot the flyer."

"There's a speech by the mayor to officially kick off the event at four. Then music by some local bands. People usually spread out and have picnics and the kids wade and swim in the lake. Then there's a boring history talk on the gargun for out-of-towners. After that, there's some more music and the fireworks. That's about it tonight."

Vic nodded.

"Chances are that if he strikes again, it won't be until dusk. It would be easier to blend in. We've got to stay on high alert though. Oh, and hey, I brought you one of these," Vic lowered his sunglasses and tossed something black at Alex who caught it one-handed.

It was a black T-shirt that said, "Backyard Films," in large, white letters.

"Now you're official," Vic said with a half-smile. His eyes were still red-rimmed and his hair looked like it had gotten caught in a lawn mower.

"Thanks, man," Alex slipped the shirt on over his other T-shirt. He didn't tell Vic that he thought his company was pretty cool. Actually, Alex had a lot of questions for Vic: like how long had he been in the film business and how much money did he make? But he didn't ask them. Alex had a feeling that Vic wasn't in the mood to answer questions and anyway, he didn't want to look like a dork.

The crowd down at the lake was even more concentrated than up on the road. Vic whistled as he looked around. Then he plunked down the backpack, dug through it, and apparently found what he was looking for.

"I'm going to get some footage. Never know—I might be producing this segment even after all that's happened. Although with Nikki and Joe…"

Alex saw his Adam's apple bob.

"Maybe it could be like a tribute episode to them," Alex offered.

Vic nodded and cleared his throat. "Yeah. Yeah, that's not a bad idea."

He hoisted the camera and tripod up and over his shoulder. Alex grabbed the bag, and they followed the crowd down to the beach. Most of the prime spots had already been nabbed by people who'd staked their claims hours earlier with camp chairs, blankets, and beach towels. Some people came in the late morning and spent the day, intent on getting the best spot for the speeches and entertainment.

"I'm going to head that way, get a panoramic," Vic said, nodding toward the left edge of the beach. Further beyond it, yellow police tape flapped in the wind, and Alex saw a few people in drab clothes standing around, consulting clipboards and talking to each other. Those must be the state detectives. Alex felt a thrum of excitement despite the reason they were there.

"Sounds good," he said. "Want me to come?"

Vic stared at the yellow tape and the state people for a few minutes. Finally, he seemed to snap out of it. "Nah," he replied. "Just don't go far. In case we need to contact Jessica and Tony. And keep your eyes out," he told Alex again.

What else would he do? Alex wondered but just nodded and turned back toward the crowd. He raised his arm to wave at a couple of guys from his soccer team and smiled at Trina Baker. She looked extra hot today, in frayed shorts and a complicated-looking strappy white top. She smiled back, her dimple deepening. But then a friend grabbed her arm and pulled her toward another group of kids from school. He was about to follow but shook his head. He was here to work. He needed to focus.

Alex had been lifeguarding at the pool for two summers now. One of the things he'd learned in training was the essential ability to block out everything that wasn't important. Early on, he'd had to force himself to block out the hot girls in bikinis who flipped their hair when they walked by, and the gross sight of fat grannies in strange swim dresses, along with seriously hairy men, and watch for what was important: was anyone struggling in the water? Did anyone look fatigued? Like they were in pain? He'd learned to pan the faces in the water, looking for facial signs that would indicate distress. He'd also learned to scan the area around the pool. Little kids loved to get close to the water without life vests on, even if they couldn't swim. And they had a way of doing it when their mothers were distracted.

Alex used those same skills now. He took a breath, lowered his shoulders, and looked around the crowd. At first glance, all you could see was movement. All you could hear was the roar of lots of voices. But Alex stilled himself and looked again. His eyes flicked over the kids from school and further out, toward the edges of the crowd. A few small food trucks had been brought in and the lines in front of them were long and straggling. Mothers wiped little kids' faces while dads tossed frisbees to older kids. There were more kids in the water, most up to their knees at least, some fully immersed. Towels and picnic blankets covered a large portion of the beachfront.

Further up the beach, toward where it turned wooded, the older crowd hung out. He recognized Janice and Billy Drey, who had been two years ahead of him in school. Other college-aged kids were dancing to the music he could barely hear and sipping from cans that sparkled in the sunlight. Further up, behind them, the crowd thinned. The sheer rock face of Gargun's Footstool rose there and beyond it the narrow strip of road with sagging guardrails. Alex scanned that area carefully. Had it been just two days ago that him and Kyle had run up it?

"Hey, Alex." He felt a powerful hand grip his shoulder and turned.

"Oh, hi Mr. Minkler," Alex said. "Enjoying the event?"

"Oh, you know. It's a must-do for summer, right?"

Alex chuckled politely. Mr. Minkler was his dad's boss and had taken a liking to Alex. "He's got real potential, Artie," he'd said to Alex's father. No one called Arthur, "Artie" except Mr. Minkler.

"Your family here?"

Alex shook his head. "No, not yet."

"What's this," Mr. Minkler nodded to Alex's shirt. "You here on official business?"

"Just helping out on a videography project. It's a documentary about the...the area."

"Good, good," Mr. Minkler said and waved to someone in the crowd. "Gotta run. The missus has the picnic ready. Good seeing you, son."

"Thanks. You too, Mr. Minkler." Alex gave a winning smile. The thought of ending up like his dad, working on salary at an accounting firm like Minkler and Co., made him feel tight and itchy. Alex certainly didn't plan to stick around Stillwater. But it never hurt to have friends in higher places. He might be able to use the man for a reference on his college applications at least.

Alex went back to scanning the cliffs. The sun cast shadows on the rockface, making it difficult to see clearly. He pulled his sunglasses off, but that just made it worse. Replacing them, he glanced back toward where Vic had gone. Alex could just see him, far off on a little knoll, panning the crowd with the big camera and started walking back that way. The smell of frying foods and something sweet made his stomach growl. His parents should be here soon. Alex hoped his mother had made extra sandwiches this year. Last year his brother had polished off the last two while Alex had been distracted by the band.

Maneuvering around a loud group of kids, Alex glanced over to the tree line where Vic stood. He blinked. A shadowy figure stood near the largest pine, looking out over the crowd. Alex squinted, trying to make sure he'd seen what he thought he had.

It was gone.

He let out a big breath and smiled to himself. Tony was right. They were starting to see the gargun everywhere. Even—

A shadowy form moved, closer to Vic now but still hidden partially by the tree line. Alex stopped walking and stared.

The figure turned slightly. Alex felt his blood turn into ice water. Two white globes stood out from the thing's head.

Alex started running.

It was the gargun.

And it was within yards of where Vic stood.

Chapter 26

Tony Bradford

Main Street was deserted, the festivities at the lake drawing everyone away from town. While finding a parking spot was easy, the historical society was closed like Jessica had feared. The library, however, was still open for another couple of hours according to the sun-faded sign on the door.

"Not closing early for the kickoff?" Tony asked the elderly woman behind the counter after they'd greeted each other. He forced himself to remain calm and easygoing. It wouldn't help to run around in a panic.

Everything about this librarian spelled seasoned from the half-glasses perched on her nose to the gray hair neatly pulled into a bun. She even wore a cardigan with a little gold chain keeping it in place over her shoulders.

"Oh, my no. I don't attend anymore. Too much drinking and cavorting for my taste," she smiled as she said it and Tony smiled back.

"Well, we're glad you're here. I'm Tony and this is my friend Jessica. We're doing some research and were hoping to look through some of the old records."

The smile on the woman's face got brighter. "Well, isn't that nice! You don't see many people in here who care about old records anymore, not unless they're doing genealogical research." She stood.

"I'm Mrs. Burbank. Come this way," she motioned to a dimly lit hallway. "I'd be happy to show you the microfiche machines. That's where we're putting all the old documents these days. It's too hard on the original documents, you see, being handled. Those are all being transferred over to the state archives." She fiddled with the sweater chain, smoothed out some imperceptible tangle.

"That's kind of you," Jessica said. "It's just, we're sort of in a hurry. We're leaving town tonight and we need to get on the road soon. Before the, uh, celebration breaks up."

"Oh." Mrs. Burbank frowned. "Well, what kind of records are you looking for?"

"It's about my, uh, mother's side of the family. We have this name—Caleb Coventry—and we're trying to find his descendants. My ancestors, I mean," Jessica said.

"I see. So, it is family research you're doing after all." The librarian sounded as though she'd just been informed her cat had been run over by a car. "Well," she squared her thin shoulders. "There's a resource book you'll find immensely helpful."

Tony and Jessica trailed the elderly librarian to the section marked, "Resource Room," a tiny closet of a space lined with very old, dusty-looking books in drab colors. She ran her finger along the spines until finding the one she wanted.

"Here we go," she pulled it free, nearly staggering under its weight. Tony leaped forward and took it for her, depositing it on the nearby table. The book must have weighed twenty pounds.

She smiled at Tony and—had she just fluttered her eyelashes, or had he imagined it?

"Now," Mrs. Burbank was slightly out of breath. "What you have here is *Betty Jarboe's Obituaries: A Guide to Sources.* This will speed up your research time considerably." She blinked up at Tony, as though he should understand why.

"Great," Tony said. "But how exactly will it help us?"

"Oh, of course." The librarian chuckled and waved a hand through the air. "I forget that not everyone has been doing this as long as me. Think of this as an index of sorts, for obituaries. Here, you can search by name, look up the obituary on the microfiche by date, and then, *voila*! Now, you will still need to use the microfiche machines—I can show you exactly how they work—but this way you'll have a much narrower window to search."

Tony let out a relieved sigh. "You're a Godsend, Mrs. B."

She let out a chuckle and winked at him. He saw Jessica's amused glance and embarrassingly, felt his cheeks redden.

"Now, you let me know if you run into trouble. I'll be re-shelving for a while longer yet."

"Someone's got an admirer," Jessica whispered, half-laughing as Mrs. Burbank wheeled her cart off around a corner.

Tony rolled up his sleeves and smiled. "Would you believe me if I told you it happens a lot with older women?"

Jessica snorted.

"Let's find Caleb."

***

It took more than an hour, but they eventually managed to

locate all the male descendants of Caleb Coventry, from the year he died until the 1950s, the last time *Betty Jarboe's Obituaries* had been updated.

"This is the last one," Jessica frowned as she read silently over Tony's shoulder. "Hiram Knobb."

A bell rang in Tony's head but then went silent when he tried to place the name. He was tired, his eyes felt like gritty sandpaper and he was long overdue for his fourth cup of coffee. "Do you want to do the honors?"

Jessica grinned. "Sure."

"Okay. I'm going to find the restroom."

Jessica nodded and began to search the boxes of neatly labeled microfiche for the right date.

Tony followed the sign for the bathroom back out into the main hallway and used the surprisingly new-looking facilities. He was about to head back into the library when he remembered the walkie-talkie. He'd turned it off by habit like he did with his cellphone when entering the library.

He turned the dial up now and listened. Nothing but silence. Holding the unit close to his face, he asked quietly, "Vic? Alex? You guys doing all right?"

There was no sound, static or otherwise to indicate that either of them had heard him. Tony had found it hard to believe any walkie-talkies would have a range like Alex was talking about. He was about to click the knob back to the off position when Alex responded, his voice high and tight.

"The gargun...here!" he panted. "It's...at the lake...hurry! ...get Vic. Near the woods...Elmer's—"

Then nothing. The walkie-talkie had completely cut out.

"Alex?"

No response.

Tony shook the unit, then smacked it against his palm a few times. Had the batteries gone?

"Alex?"

Nothing.

"Alex, you there?"

Still no response.

Leaving the walkie-talkie's volume up, Tony jogged back into the library.

Jessica stood over the microfiche machine as a paper whirred out from it. She raised her eyebrows when she saw Tony.

"We need to go," Tony's voice was an urgent whisper. "There's a...situation down at the lake."

"Okay." The smile fell away as she shoved the papers at him. "But Tony, you're not going to believe this. Look right there," she jabbed at an obituary about halfway down the page. "Death Notice," it said in bold print, and then, "Hiram Knobb".

Hiram Knobb is survived by his wife, Patricia Kearns Knobb of twenty-seven years, along with the couple's only child, Harlan Knobb. The family wishes to thank the community at large for its support during this difficult time...

"The paper's from nineteen sixty-eight. And that's the most recent mention of Caleb's descendants in the news. He might still be alive! Oh, and another thing."

"What?" Tony helped Jessica hurriedly gather the reels of film and put them back into the box.

"Harlan Knobb doesn't have any kids."

"How do you know that?"

"Because I found another article, oh, where is it?" she fumbled through the small stack she'd printed. "Here!" She held it up victoriously. "He won an award as a history professor, and it mentions that he never married or had children."

"Knobb. That's where the bell was coming from," Tony said.

"What?"

"Nothing. I'll explain on the way."

Over loud *thank-yous* to Mrs. Burbank, they ran out the door to Tony's Jeep. He tossed the walkie-talkie in Jessica's lap and gunned the engine.

"Try to get Alex. He said that the gargun is there. Vic's in trouble."

Chapter 27

Alex Richards

T he forest around Alex creaked, sighed, and groaned. It was like a living thing, moving, talking, listening.

He gave himself a mental shake. *Chill. It's just the woods.*

But these woods felt different, ominous. Because he'd seen the gargun go into them. Any second, Alex expected one of the thing's gray hands to slip out from behind a tree, or to find Vic pinned against one with a knife in his chest. Alex's mouth was pasty when he swallowed. He wanted to call out for Vic. But then the gargun would know right where he was.

This was like the start of every summer camp horror movie he'd ever seen. Boy separated from group. Strange sounds. Creepy music. Then—Alex looked around him wildly.

Chill. He had to chill, not freak out like a little girl.

He adjusted his damp grip on the handle of the knife. It wasn't his first choice of a weapon, but he hadn't found the key to his father's pistol case. His dad moved it around frequently, worried that Alex's little brother would find it. Alex wished with a sudden intensity that his father was here. He also wished he'd seen one of the detectives, but they'd all disappeared when

Vic had gone into the woods, with that thing following behind him—

A branch broke to his left. Alex whirled in that direction; knife held high.

Nothing there.

The sun dappled through the leaves and other than the normal noises of the woods, he couldn't hear anything.

Where had the gargun gone? And how could it move so silently through the forest while dragging along a grown man? Unless it hadn't caught Vic. Yet.

Or unless Vic was dead.

A crow cawed overhead, and Alex jumped. The bird lifted off the branch so close to his head that he heard the air moving through its long, black feathers.

The ground grew steeper. Alex paused by an outcropping of rocks and looked around but stayed close to the stones. Vic—if he was still alive—and the gargun could be anywhere. There were big pine trees with low branches, perfect to hide under. More groups of boulders like this one were scattered over this part of the woods. Alex craned his neck to look above and saw an opening in the stones.

What was that? A cave? It had been years since Alex had hiked here but he didn't remember it.

Pushing off from the rocks, Alex climbed toward the dark hole. His heart hammered in his chest. If the cave was empty, it would be a good place to hide. Alex could wait for the gargun to show himself. Or maybe it was nearby, watching and waiting for Alex to pass by. He shivered, goosebumps stampeding down his arms and legs. He thought of Kyle and the bruises and cuts and his strangely crushed skull and the mark on him.

Nope. Nope, nope.

He had to focus, keep his bearings.

To the right of the cave's entrance was a flat area, smooth and covered with pine needles. Alex saw a flash of orange and paused. What was that? Something Vic had dropped? He tried to remember if he'd had something in his hands, what he'd been wearing even, but couldn't remember anything other than the camera and tripod. He was sure that's all Vic had had with him. He climbed up closer for a better look.

An orange backpack—the kind you'd find at the expensive camping stores, lay on its side. Alex hesitated, glanced behind him again.

It would be easy to slip away. He could find his parents or cut through the woods and make it back to his house without anyone seeing him. He didn't really know Vic. And he was just a teenager, not some superhero. Even if he found Vic and the gargun had him, what could Alex do? He twisted the switch on the walkie-talkie and listened but only heard soft static.

Something moved in the woods downhill. Branches broke. Alex heard the rustle of leaves.

He looked wildly in that direction.

The gargun was coming. He couldn't see it yet but he could hear it climbing up toward him.

There was a sharp pressure in his chest—like someone had reached their hand in and squeezed—and it was suddenly hard to breathe.

Alex wasn't going to wait around for the gargun to pick him off. He dove off the trail and into the forest, headed back down to the lake. He skirted a patch of poisonous parsnip and leaped over a fallen log. He didn't bother to try and be quiet any longer. His feet thundered and the brush all around him shook as he plunged deeper into the undergrowth. He'd skirt the area where he'd heard the noise, jump back on the trail lower down, and run back to the crowded beach. He'd find his father, get help. Or maybe just keep running until he was far away from Stillwater.

He was nearly back to the trail, could see the thin ribbon of brown to his left. Alex shoved his way through a thick, sprawling bush.

He collided with someone. A hand gripped his arm and Alex yelled.

"Shh, it's me," a soft voice whispered. The other hand snaked out of the bush and pushed aside the branches so he could see.

"What are you doing here?" Alex asked Lydia. His breath came in short, jerky gasps.

"I followed you. Is it here?" She craned her neck, tried to see around Alex, her eyes wide.

"I came in after Vic. The gargun…I think it's hunting him."

"I know. I saw you—called to you before you ran in here, but you didn't stop."

"I didn't hear you," Alex's breath was still coming in gasps.

"You didn't find Vic?" Lydia whispered.

"No. I found a pack though."

"Was it his?"

"No, it's orange. It's up there," he nodded his head back toward the direction he'd come. "Someone must have left it. Maybe camping. Do you have any water?"

"No, sorry." Lydia chewed her lip. "That's weird. Why would someone leave their pack?" Then, "Let's go."

Relief washed over Alex. Now he could tell everyone that he'd had to leave because Lydia had been scared.

"Okay," he said and moved past her downhill.

"Where are you going?"

Alex stopped mid-stride.

"I mean, let's go and find Vic. He needs us, Alex. We can't just leave him out here to die."

Why couldn't they, Alex thought. They barely knew the guy. But he said, "Sure, uh, I know. I was just checking behind you, making sure the gargun wasn't lurking around back here."

"Gee thanks." Lydia's voice was sarcastic.

Alex blinked. He'd been surprised that she'd come after him and Vic in the first place. And now she was all salty about it.

Lydia climbed the rest of the way through the branches and dusted herself off quickly. "Show me the pack. Maybe we can find some clues as to where the hiker went. Maybe he or she will lead us to Vic."

They retraced Alex's earlier path and inspected the pack, but Lydia said they shouldn't take time to get everything out. They found some imprints of hiking boots on the soft ground but only a couple near the backpack.

"Besides, whoever owns it might not be far away." She frowned, glanced around at the thick tree cover and tangled undergrowth. "It's probably better if we split up."

"No way."

She glanced at him her eyebrows raised.

"I don't think that would be safe. I mean, you don't even have a weapon, do you?" Alex put a hand protectively on the handle of the knife on his belt.

Lydia stooped and picked up a thick branch. "Now I do."

"It's still not a good idea. We should stay together."

She nodded. "All right," she said. "My dad said when you're doing search and rescue, it's best to make circles—larger and larger—until you find whoever it is you're looking for."

"I thought your dad was a volunteer firefighter."

"He was. But he started in search and rescue—when he was

in college."

"Okay. Whatever."

"Let's start over there. Where the boot prints are," Lydia said softly and pointed toward the woods to the far right of the little clearing. Alex shrugged and followed her. His heart still pounded hard, and his hand was slippery on the knife. But he was relieved too. Embarrassed but relieved to not be out here alone.

"Where did Tony and Jessica go?" Lydia asked in a loud whisper.

"The historical society to look up town records."

She nodded. "I wonder if they—" Lydia's words morphed into a scream. The shrill sound filled the air. Then she flung herself backward, into Alex. Turned and buried her face in his shoulder.

"Oh no. No, no, no—" Her voice was half shriek, half moan.

Alex wanted to ask, What? What is it? But couldn't get his mouth to move.

Lydia didn't answer. He pushed past her, shoved aside the branches she'd been walking through.

Before him, on the ground, lay a blond man with bulging eyes. His entire chest was stained red and so was the bed of pine needles underneath him. Alex turned away, prayed he wouldn't be sick.

Nearby a branch broke. He and Lydia both looked wildly in that direction. A shadowy figure crouched by a tree. Alex's first thought was, "run!".

Lydia screamed again. The figure didn't move. Was it the gargun? The darkness of the tree branches made it impossible to tell.

Alex plunged back into the woods the way they'd come.

Out. Out. He had to get out of here.

Lydia cried out. "Alex!"

He slowed.

"Alex!"

It had gotten her. It had grabbed Lydia and was going to kill her. He felt the same panic wash over him that he'd felt that night at Gargun's Footstool. The fear, bitter in his mouth, added fuel to his legs.

"Please!" Her voice was faint now and he heard another sound. Had it been a shout or a tree branch? It was hard to hear over the pulse that pounded in his ears.

He kept running.

He couldn't. He couldn't go back. It would get him too.

But how could he leave Lydia there, to die? With a grunt, he changed directions, headed back the way he'd come.

Lydia kneeled on the ground, close to the dark huddled figure. It must have grabbed her. It was holding onto her.

Remembering the knife suddenly, Alex unclasped it and drew it over his head. He was about to plunge it into the unmoving head of the gargun when Lydia grabbed his arm and shoved it away.

"Don't! It's Vic."

It was like trying to make out what someone was saying underwater. Vic? Alex lowered the knife, sank onto his haunches. He was so close to Lydia that he could smell the faint scent of her shampoo.

"He's...he's dead I think." She put a hand over her mouth like she was trying to hold in a sob. Or vomit.

Alex pushed in front of her to see Vic more closely. He was slumped against the tree, like someone who'd had too much to drink and had passed out. His body was turned away from them, the dark shirt and black jeans making him more of an outline than a person from this angle.

"We're too late," Lydia whispered.

Two thoughts ran simultaneously through Alex's head. That they should get out of here now. Vic was dead so there was no sense in being in the woods any longer. The other thought was more a sensation. That they were being watched.

"Let's go," Alex said, his voice a whisper.

"Wait, let me see," Lydia held out a shaking hand toward Vic.

"What are you doing?"

"We should check his pulse. Maybe he's just unconscious."

Lydia reached out a hand and gripped Vic's shoulder. Then she pulled, rolling him back toward them. His chin which had rested on his chest lolled to the side. His shirt was two shades of black—the faded T-shirt with the Backyard Films logo a soot shade around his chest. Lydia flinched when she saw that.

"Blood," she pointed to the ground around him where droplets ran into the crushed ferns and dead leaves. She reached for his wrist and pressed her fingers there.

"He has a pulse," Lydia turned back to Alex. "He's got a pulse, Alex." She smiled. "He's alive!"

"Okay, good, great." Alex sat back on his haunches. His mind felt like oatmeal, and it was hard to make thoughts work in order. "How are we going to get him out of here?"

"We can't. Not by ourselves. Go get that pack. We can find something in there to stop the bleeding and then go and get help."

Alex returned a minute later with the bright orange bag which they opened and dumped upside down. All the regular camping and hiking things fell out—rope and a tin pot, a small camp stove, plastic containers full of food and coffee, a tent painstakingly folded and compressed.

"There, give me that," Lydia snatched at a piece of long underwear. "It'll work. Can you find me a thick cloth or a shirt—something we can use to stop the bleeding."

Alex dug through the supplies until he found a small towel, probably for a camp kitchen. He handed it to Lydia. Without a word, she pressed the folded towel against the wound in Vic's chest. He moaned but didn't open his eyes.

"Hold that in place."

Alex hesitated. He wanted to puke but did what she said. Once his hands were in place, Lydia snaked the long underwear over the cloth with the feet ends pointed towards Vic's back.

"Help me lay him down," Lydia shook Alex's arm. He looked at her but felt strange. Like she was on the other side of a football field. He could hardly hear her. He shook his head and tried to clear it.

"What?"

"Help me get him on the ground. I'll be able to keep better pressure if he's laying down."

"How do you know all this stuff?" His lips felt numb.

"I watch a lot of TV. Come on, help me."

Together, they carefully moved Vic onto his side under the tree. Fresh blood oozed out of his chest and Alex gagged and looked away. Lydia tied the long underwear firmly in place over the towel that hid the gaping hole in Vic. She had enough length to bring the legs of the long johns back to the front and knot them over the towel. More blood oozed out when she pulled it tight, but then seemed to stop.

I'm never eating steak again, Alex thought, as the edges of his vision went gray.

"Okay, that should be good enough for now." Lydia's hands

were red with blood, but she didn't seem to notice. "Did you try the walkie-talkie?" She had tiny splatters of red on her face and her breath was coming too fast, in little hitching sounds. Her eyes were very wide and her skin was very pale.

"Yeah. It's not working in here. There must be too many shrees. I mean, trees." Alex forced himself to look away from Vic before he threw up.

"One of us needs to go get help. You're a faster runner, do you want to?"

"Okay," Alex said. He wanted to tell Lydia that he was afraid he might never stop running once he started, but kept his mouth shut.

"Keep this," he handed her the walkie-talkie. "Maybe Tony or Jessica will call."

"Hurry. He's losing a lot of blood."

There was a noise—something far away and down below them maybe? The carpeting of the forest and the tangled undergrowth muted the sound.

Then closer, branches broke. Footsteps pounded.

Trees and leaves and bushes shook. Whatever it was it was big and coming closer.

"Run!" Alex whispered and pushed Lydia in the opposite direction of the footsteps.

Chapter 28

Jessica Brown

E lmer's, it turned out wasn't a store or restaurant, but a mountain trail. The official name was Elmer's Point but she thought it had been misnamed. Maybe Death Trail or I'll Kill You Vista would have been a better choice. The map had called the trail "difficult" but that was the understatement of the year.

"This way," Jessica looked frantically from the tourist map in Tony's vehicle to the beachfront.

Traffic down to the lake had been horrible and they'd finally had to leave the Jeep parked awkwardly and likely illegally, before sprinting toward the lake. At least, they'd tried to sprint. In the end, they'd jostled and shoved their way through groups of friends and family. Despite Tony's loud, "excuse us," and "pardon us," they'd gotten many hostile glares and a few exclamations of surprise. Once, they nearly knocked down a kid. Another time they'd narrowly avoided a big guy who looked like he could eat them for breakfast…simultaneously.

They'd crisscrossed the open meadow, ignored the crime scene tape that fluttered further down the beach, and jogged straight up a dirt trail that led into the thick forest beyond.

"There it is," Jessica called over her shoulder, pointing at the green sign labeled, "Elmer's Point," in faded letters. An arrow pointed in the direction they were going. Jessica ran faster, Tony right behind her. The path was too narrow for them to stay two abreast, and when Jessica tired a bit further up, Tony took the lead.

"You all right?" he asked, barely breathing hard.

"Yes," she gasped. "Just realizing now how much better it is to get a gym membership and use it than carry the card around."

They focused on the trail for a few yards. It was rocky and rutted. Tree roots poked in and out of its surface and made the going slow.

"We need a plan," Tony called over his shoulder. She could faintly smell his aftershave or deodorant. "And we need to stick together."

"The chances of me arguing that are nil," Jessica panted. The incline was still steep, but not as bad as the start where it'd felt like she was running up the side of a wall. Damn her and her cigarettes. She was done. Absolutely done, no more smoking for her. Ever.

"Should we call for them?" she asked, trying, and failing to keep a wheeze out of her voice.

Tony shook his head. "No, but let's keep trying the radio."

Jessica tapped it against Tony's shoulder, and he slowed down enough to grab it from her.

"Alex? Vic? Do you read me?"

Nothing.

They'd had to slow to a fast hike, running was impossible here. The uneven ground and narrow winding path were treacherous.

Tony adjusted a button, glancing between the walkie-talkie and the ground, then tried again.

"Vic? Alex?"

Silence on the other end.

"I don't get why he would have turned it off." Jessica huffed. "Unless he dropped it somewhere."

Or unless the gargun took it from them, Jessica thought but didn't say it aloud.

The ground rose steeply again, and Jessica felt like her heart was about to jump directly out of her chest and onto the ground in front of her. A stitch had formed in her right side, like a knife being jabbed between her ribs. She put a hand there and pushed on it. Her calves burned like lava had replaced the blood in her veins.

She looked around the woods, certain she'd see a hulking gray figure behind every thick tree. It would be so easy to miss someone. This felt like true wilderness. The trees were thick and the undergrowth off the trail was choking. Shadows and gloom hung everywhere. Big boulders were embedded into the side of the mountain. Many of the trees were coated with thick moss and surrounded by a lot of plants Jessica didn't recognize. It was like they'd been sucked into one of Grimm's Fairytales. You could almost see Hansel and Gretel's breadcrumb trail and the peak of a gingerbread house roof—

A scream punctuated the air. Tony and Jessica both stopped, mid-stride and stared at each other.

"What direction?"

Jessica shook her head. "I think…" she panted. Then gave up and pointed up and to the right.

Tony nodded. "You okay?"

She nodded and made a "go on," motion with her hands.

"Alex? Vic?" Tony tried the walkie-talkie again, his voice tight and low. "Come in, guys. We're here. At Elmer's Point. Guys?"

Nothing.

They ran again, toward where Jessica thought the scream had come from.

"Alex!" A voice cried out. Tony stopped so abruptly that Jessica bumped into him.

"Which—"

"Alex!" The voice yelled again. It was female, scared.

Tony and Jessica plunged into the thick undergrowth. Seconds later, it fell away, into a small clearing. Just beyond it, Jessica saw snatches of color.

"It's you." Alex emerged from the tangled undergrowth. He held the branches back and a scratched up, scared-looking Lydia emerged. Her hands and arms were bloody.

"Oh my God, are you okay?" Jessica opened her arms and Lydia nearly fell into them.

"It's not me." Lydia shook her head. "It's not my blood."

"What happened? Are you all right?" Tony asked.

"Vic, he's hurt. We have to get a doctor or get him to the hospital, but I don't know how the ambulance will get through these crowds—"

"Slow down, Lydia," Tony's voice was calm but authoritative. "Where is Vic?"

"He's under a tree—back that way," Alex jerked his head back toward the forest. "And there's another guy too, but—"

"He's dead." Lydia's voice was thin.

Jessica gasped.

"Can you show us?" Tony put a hand on Alex's shoulder.

Alex nodded but didn't move. Lydia took a deep breath and walked back the way they'd come, parting the saplings and tall undergrowth with her arms.

"The gargun followed Vic in here and then Alex followed

them and I came in after them." Lydia's voice was quiet, her footsteps careful.

"We tried calling you on the walkie," Tony said, holding branches out of the way so that they wouldn't snap back in Jessica's face. "But we couldn't get you."

"It won't work up here," Alex's voice trembled. Jessica couldn't imagine how scared and exhausted they both must have been. Must be.

"As soon as we're with Vic, you two need to get out of here, go back to your parents. Tony can go with you both and call an ambulance." She looked over Lydia's head to Tony, questioning the plan with her eyes.

He nodded. "Absolutely."

Vic was lying on his side with a makeshift tourniquet tied around his chest diagonally. Tony and Lydia squatted beside him, but Alex hung back with Jessica.

"Did you do this?" Tony motioned to the bandage. Lydia nodded. "You did a really good job."

Leaning forward, he checked Vic's pulse. "It's faint, but it's there," he said. He stood, dusting his hands together.

"We need to—"

A branch beyond Tony broke, the loud crack made Jessica jump. The little group froze, then turned simultaneously like a group of marionettes. A shadowy figure crouched near a giant pine tree, maybe twenty feet from where they stood.

Slowly, the shadow peeled itself away from the tree, then glided as though in slow motion toward them. Jessica knew she had to move, get in front of the kids. But her legs wouldn't work.

Tony stepped forward toward the dark shape, blocking it from both Lydia and Alex.

The figure hesitated.

"We know who you are. No need to bother with the Halloween costume now," Tony's voice was low.

The figure jerked to a stop, turned its head toward the right. Jessica could see it more clearly now. It was the same height as a man with narrow shoulders. Its body was covered with dark black and gray robes, tattered and torn in places. In place of hands swinging near its sides, it had long, talon-like claws. And its head—she couldn't look away. Its face was gray and rubbery looking. Its eyes bulged grotesquely, like the dead frogs they'd had to dissect in tenth-grade science class. The creature's head was covered in the hood of the robe, but the way the hood made a peak made Jessica think its skull was pointed underneath. Black lines skimmed its face. She was horrified and couldn't stop looking.

"We know who you are," Tony's voice cut through the silence of the woods. "We've called the police."

The creature's head swung upright again. Then it bared its teeth—long, yellowed fangs—and Jessica couldn't breathe. Halloween costumes don't do that, Tony, she wanted to say.

Tony took an involuntary step back, and ran into Lydia and Alex. He pushed them back with his arms. They were getting closer to Vic now. Had the gargun slashed Vic with its talons? Jessica wondered. Protectively, she put out her arm, pushing Lydia further back behind herself. Now, Tony and she made up the point of an arrow, Lydia, and Alex safely behind them. Or maybe not so safely, Jessica thought.

"You're not getting these kids. Or us," Tony's voice was clear and loud. Jessica had the strange urge to cheer him on like a cheerleader at a football game. He was so calm. Her knees shook and her vision trembled. She forced herself to take regular breaths. She couldn't hyperventilate out here, pass out.

The creature made a sound then, something like a groaning growl. It started to levitate. It rose six inches, then twelve. Jessica stared, her mouth open. This absolutely can't be happening, she thought. She wanted to close her eyes, block out what she was seeing.

Tony swallowed; his Adam's apple jerked up once.

"It's not human," he said almost to himself. "It's not human. It's a demon." He crouched, as though he were about to spring at the gargun.

But the monster moved first. Quickly, the gargun rushed Tony, a screech like metal against metal booming from its open mouth. Jessica screamed and raised her hands to her ears, wishing she had a gun, a knife, a tree branch to protect herself with. Then, remembering something, she dug into the pocket of her shorts.

Tony yelled, barely audibly over the gargun's screech. They collided, their bodies smashing together, bodies tangled, grunting and panting. They fell to the needle-strewn floor of the forest. Tony yelled in pain and Jessica saw a bright red line of blood flow from the back of his ripped shirt. She stared wild-eyed at the scene before she jerked herself from her stupor and grabbed the pink tube of pepper spray from her pocket. She aimed at the creature, but it was too hard to separate it from Tony. Then the gargun made that sound again—a metallic screech so loud she wanted to clamp her hands over her ears. It reared back as Tony shouted—

"…in the name…Jesus Christ…command you…come out—"

The creature bellowed as like Tony had run it through with a sword. It didn't stop struggling though as Tony continued. Its groans and screeches made it impossible to hear everything

Tony was saying, only snatches of his words.

"...shadow of this world..." and then "...get behind me..." The creature thrashed as if Tony had struck it with an electrical prod.

"No power greater...the one true God and..."

The gargun screamed again and collapsed onto the ground writhing. Its back was pinned to the earth but its legs and long arms flailed against the ground. Tony had gotten close to it—too close, Jessica thought—and stood over it with his hand outstretched The glint of a silver crucifix flashed from the neck opening of his shirt. The simple cross swung on a thin leather cord.

The gargun screamed again, its body jerking and spasming under the robes. Its big head rolled to one side, then the other. There was another sound too, like water rushing toward them. It became so loud, that Jessica looked around them. She expected to see a wall of water crashing down the mountainside toward them.

But there was nothing there.

The sky overhead grew dark, storm clouds rolling and twisting, pressed up tightly against the trees, covering their tops.

Tony kept going. It sounded like he was quoting from the Bible Jessica thought, though it had been a very long time since she'd been to her grandmother's little brown church.

The gargun twisted and moaned. Its mouth was open, white foamy spittle dripping from between its teeth. Its bulging eyes seemed to bulge even further out. The sound of rushing water, Jessica realized, was coming from the creature.

"...in the name of the Father, Son, and Holy Spirit...I command—"

There was a single piercing shriek, followed by what sounded like hundreds of others. Jessica clamped her hands over her ears, dropping her pepper spray on the ground. It bounced harmlessly on a stone and rolled away. The creature shook so violently that the bushes and trees nearby shook. Even the ground underneath Jessica's feet jittered. Small stones skidded downhill toward them, and trees trembled as though caught in a huge storm.

Then, a blinding white light—an explosion of brightness—faded to a blue glow that covered the creature. It lay still on the ground.

Tony was panting, hands on his knees as he shook his head slowly from side to side. Tears ran down his face and Jessica wanted to go to him, wrap an arm around him, comfort him. But she was frozen in place. She watched as he sank to his knees and put his head in his hands. He stared at the creature, awe and shock painted onto his face.

The blueish light around the gargun faded. And then tiny pinpricks of light slowly began to rise from its collapsed body. One, then two together. Three simultaneously rose upward followed by another single droplet of light followed by four more. She watched without breathing, as the bright, tiny orbs rose upward into the sky that had turned dark. They looked like miniature stars, she thought. Jessica watched until they were no longer visible overhead.

Chapter 29

Tony Bradford

When the last tiny light had risen and faded away, the dark clouds parted. A beam of sunshine fell in the woods, illuminating Tony. He sank back on his feet, still kneeling, and raised his wet face toward the sky, his eyes closed. His chest was filled with incredible peace. And suddenly, for some reason he couldn't describe, he felt a bubble of deep happiness rise. A wide smile formed on his face and Tony laughed. When he opened his eyes, Jessica stood next to him. Tentatively, she put a hand on his shoulder.

He jumped up, grabbed her in a hug, and squeezed her so hard that he lifted her from the ground.

"It's over," he said. "It's over." The joy in his chest grew instead of fading. He wanted to dance her around in a circle, sing, and whoop all at the same time.

"What…" She started but then stopped and put her hands on either side of his face. "You're amazing."

He shook his head. "Not me. I'm just the messenger."

"You saved us."

"No," he laughed and tugged her hands down into his. "That was the Big Guy upstairs." He glanced above them. Jessica looked up too.

Tony hugged her again and looked toward the figure on the ground.

"Look," he said, some of the happy glow fading. "It's Harlan Knobb. Just like we thought."

Jessica turned to see for herself. The gray and black robes were in a heap on the ground. Instead of the large gray figure with bulging eyes, though, a thin, pale man lay in the fabric. His mouth was slightly open, his eyes were closed.

"Is he...?"

"Dead? I don't think so," Tony moved toward the man, but Jessica held him back.

"No, don't."

"I have to see." Tony's voice was gentle as he let go of her hands and moved toward the man on the ground.

"That...that's Mr. Knobb. He owns the bed and breakfast in town," Lydia's voice was shaky. Jessica had nearly forgotten she and Alex were there with everything happening.

"Are you okay?" Jessica moved to Lydia and wrapped an arm around her shoulders. Alex was hunched over, hands on his knees, staring at the ground.

"He's still breathing," Tony said. His finger was pressed into Harlan's neck. It was thin and pale, Jessica thought, completely unlike the gargun's thick, ropy gray one.

"We need to call an ambul—"

Suddenly, Harlan's hand shot up from his side and grabbed Tony around the neck. Jessica gasped and instinctively stepped back. The heel of her shoe caught on a root and she nearly fell, would have if Lydia hadn't steadied her. She stared dumbly, horrified by the scene.

Harlan had sat up halfway, his fingers digging into Tony's

throat like daggers. She could see the tips white against Tony's reddening face. He made a strange gurgling sound and then swung his arm at Harlan. The punch connected solidly with Harlan's cheek and made a horrible, hollow sound, and then his pale face jerked sideways.

Lydia had never seen someone punched like that in real life. In the movies, it was all over so quickly and the person getting hit usually popped back up immediately and took another punch. But Mr. Knobb just lay there, breathing hard. A little drool came out of his mouth and formed strings into the dirt under his head.

"Someone throw me the rope," Tony said. Jessica scrambled to her feet and dug through the pile of camping supplies until she found a coil of blue rope. She gave it to Tony with shaking hands.

"Are you all right?"

He nodded, grunting as he bound Harlan's hands behind his back.

Minutes later, Harlan lay on his stomach, spitting dirt from his bloodied mouth and cursing under his breath. Tony wrapped his arms around Jessica and she sank into his embrace. His shirt was hot and damp, his hair she noticed when she put her hands in it, was coated with sticky pine pitch.

"Guys?" Lydia called. "Alex doesn't look good."

They broke apart immediately.

"Alex?" Tony moved closer just in time to catch the teen as he fell to the ground.

"I got you. Careful there, big guy." He settled Alex with his back against a tree.

"Did we really...did we just see all that for real?" Lydia asked, pulling away from Jessica. "I mean—did that really just happen?"

Jessica nodded.

"But why—Mr. Knobb?" Lydia asked. "Why would he do that?"

"He was a descendant of Caleb Coventry," Jessica suddenly felt very, very tired. She cleared her throat. "The last descendant."

"And he—he transformed somehow?"

"*Poltergeist*," Alex muttered, his head still down between his knees. "I told you guys."

"We'll probably never really understand how it all happened. But the oath, the curse, whatever you want to call it allowed the gargun—or a spirit that made itself into the gargun—to take over a human body. Amazing," Tony shook his head.

"Not the word I'd use," Jessica laughed shakily. "Terrifying. Unbelievably horrible, yes. But amazing? Not so much."

A groan sounded from beyond where Alex rested against the tree.

"Vic," Tony and Jessica hurried back to the spot where the man was laying, Lydia trailed behind.

"Let's get you out of here," Tony said. "Let's all get out of here."

Chapter 30

Lydia Donovan

T he hours following their leaving the woods were a
blur to Lydia. She remembered how surreal it had
felt, stumbling out of the woods and seeing the festival
going on. The loud music and bright lights from kids' toys
dotting the crowd had made her a little dizzy at first.

Alex and Jessica had gone for help, returning what felt like
hours later with EMTs who got Vic onto a backwoods stretcher.
Mr. Knobb had been forced to walk, escorted by two cops.
More had been placed in the area, protecting the dead man she
and Alex had found.

She hadn't seen Alex since everything happened. When
Jessica gave her a ride home, she'd asked if Lydia had wanted to
stop by and see him before going home.

"No, thanks."

"You sure?"

Lydia nodded. She thought about her belief that being Alex's
girlfriend would change her life. She thought about Mr. Knobb
and the secrets that he'd harbored for so long. And she thought
about her parents and life here in Stillwater. It was easy to
only see the bad stuff. But when this was over and things were

back to normal, Lydia decided, she was going to start looking at things differently. Life, love, challenges—everything.

Walking in her front door was the best feeling of her life. Her mother, face stained with tears, sat on the old blue couch, a pile of damp tissues at her feet. She'd flown across the room, grabbing Lydia in her arms and hugging her so hard Lydia half-expected her head to pop free of her shoulders.

"Oh my God, Lydia! Where have you been? I've been calling everyone—I couldn't reach most of them. I went down to the lake, but it was impossible down there and I thought you'd come here and—Oh, Doogle!"

Her mother had pulled away to look at her but hugged her tight again. Lydia didn't resist. She hugged her right back.

"Are you okay? What happened?"

"You should be very proud of your daughter," Jessica said from the doorway. "She saved a man's life tonight."

"She—what?"

For the first time, her mother really seemed to look at Lydia. Her bloodstained arms, her ripped clothes, the twigs, and dead leaves snarled in her hair.

She sank to the couch, her face pale.

"It's all right, Mom. I'm fine now." Lydia sat beside her.

She glanced at Jessica who gave her a small wave. "I'm going to go find Tony. We'll check in on you both tomorrow, okay?"

Penny stared at her dumbly, so Lydia nodded. "Okay. Thank you."

"Start at the beginning," her mother said when she'd finally seemed to get her bearings. "Tell me everything that happened."

***

Hours later, exhausted but too wired to sleep, Lydia sat on the back porch and looked at the stars. She used to love to look through the big telescope her grandfather had given her when she turned twelve. Lydia felt homesick suddenly, wishing that time was a place you could go back and visit. She imagined her grandfather sitting beside her now; her hand warm in his, his breath ruffling her hair.

On Main Street, a group of kids laughed. She heard her mother on the phone in the kitchen, telling her Aunt Margaret in Cincinnati everything that had happened. Lydia had spent about an hour insisting that she hadn't been hurt and didn't need to go to the hospital. All she'd wanted, she told her mother, was a hot shower and something to eat that wasn't hot dogs. Her mother had laughed and made Lydia's favorite, tomato soup and buttery grilled cheese which Lydia had eaten two of.

She'd thought of calling Katie before her mother got on the phone but came out here instead. Somehow, she'd known this was what she needed. The soft, summer air washed over her, clearing her head of the last few hours. She heard the loud booms as the last of the fireworks exploded over Stillwater Lake. It could make her feel left out, she thought, as she curled her toes around the rough board of the stairs, but it didn't. Instead, Lydia felt very, very grateful to be exactly where she was.

Chapter 31

Deputy Gerald Pepper
Two months later

G erald sighed and ran a hand over his face. It had been a long couple of months. No, make that an exceptionally long couple of months. Leaning his arms on the desk blocked out the view of the book underneath. And that was fine. He needed a break from staring at it.

The initial trial date was finally set. Harlan Knobb would plead insanity. The two out-of-towners, Jessica Brown and Tony Bradford, were driving in next week to testify. Who'd have thought that their little town had hosted the famous Claudia Snow, aka Jessica Brown, without anyone knowing?

Life in Stillwater had been a frenzied media circus in the weeks directly following the news of the murders and the subsequent investigation by state officials. The families of the wealthy hikers had called in the troops, along with a team of private investigators who were supposed to be helping gather information, but more often got in the authorities' way. They'd been spoken to more than once and threatened with jail time if they didn't shape up. The families had also hired a couple of crackerjack lawyers.

Gerald shook his head. He wouldn't want to be in Harlan's shoes now for any money in the world. The charges against him were for six counts of murder, the attempted murder of four others, along with stalking charges and even racketeering. His role on the Stillwater Lake Festival's board as the owner of a local business and his involvement in the crimes of the gargun...well, it all seemed a little farfetched to Gerald, but he knew that the attorneys were looking for anything they could get their hands on.

Harlan Knobb's attorney would have her work cut out for her. Not only were there the witness statements but there was DNA evidence at two scenes—the death of Kyle Lanphere and the Vanders—to link Knobb to his victims. Additionally, Gerald had heard that Knobb was singing like a canary to ghostwriters, intent on getting his version of the story told in the form of a biography, as soon as the trial was over. The trouble was his story made absolutely no sense. It was like listening to the babble of a frightened toddler at best, or someone very disconnected from reality at worst. So the plead of insanity his lawyer had insisted on had stuck.

What a mess. Gerald shook his head again. If Sheriff Rinko had been around to deal with all this, what would he have thought of it? It was hard to picture the sedate, bumbling sheriff jumping through all the rings and trying not to get stuck in the red tape that Gerald had been dealing with for the past several weeks.

Thinking of the sheriff drew Gerald's gaze back to the book on the desk. It was the ledger, one of the pieces he'd borrowed from the state team to look at one more time. He ran a finger over the list of initials and the corresponding numbers. Harlan Knobb was last on the list, but he'd never had a chance to enter in his final tally. Gerald hesitated, then picked up a fountain pen that had been his uncle's and carefully wrote the number "six" under the list of other numbers.

"Is it true Harlan Knobb has no children?" One of the reporters had asked at a press conference held shortly after the state officials had arrived on the scene.

While the answer had been simply a "no comment" from the lead detective, Gerald and everyone else in town knew the answer. There was no son to carry on the Knobb name. Everyone in the area had seemed to release an extra-long breath at that reminder. The curse was over now. The pact Jenson Briggs had made with the devil all those years ago had been broken.

Except Gerald knew otherwise.

He took a sip of too-cold coffee and slid a finger over the empty line underneath Harlan Knobbs' name. He knew what would appear there next. That tiny white box would change his destiny.

"No," Harlan would say if he were sitting here now. "You did that the night that you agreed."

Had Gerald made the wrong decision? He'd been so desperate for his chance at sheriff. Had put off his dream for so many years, living in Rinko's wake. It had been easy to imagine helping his uncle. Harlan had asked so little of Gerald and his family over the years. And although during this very public trial, Gerald hadn't been able to offer Harlan much hope, he'd done what he could.

He'd met with his uncle shortly after his arrest, a private meeting in a tiny conference room that the jail housed.

"Are you okay?" Gerald had asked his uncle, realizing how stupid a question it was as soon as he'd asked it.

Harlan had laughed mirthlessly. "Just great."

"Sorry." There had been an uncomfortable silence. Then, "Can I get you anything?"

"Besides a damn good lawyer?" Harlan had asked. But then, seeing Gerald's face, softened slightly. "Maybe a cup of coffee that doesn't taste like yesterday's bathwater."

He'd done it. And then the two men had talked like they hadn't since before Rinko had died.

"It's up to you now you know," Harlan had said, cradling the paper cup and looking at Gerald. "It's on your shoulders."

Gerald had nodded slowly.

"I know."

"I hope you do a better job than I did." Harlan had shaken his head, as though filled with remorse. Was he? Gerald had wondered but hadn't asked. And if so, what did he regret—the killings or the fact that he hadn't finished his duty?

"Don't get sloppy or greedy. Study the book and learn the rules. You'll be fine," Harlan had said.

That was the last time Gerald had spoken privately with his uncle. And while he'd done his best to alter the evidence and bring doubt into the minds of those working on the case—even the townspeople, when he had the chance—Gerald didn't have hope that his efforts would be effective in helping Harlan.

What Gerald could do—the only thing now really—was to carry on his uncle's mission. No, his family's mission. Gerald didn't have a choice.

In twenty-five years, he would be sixty-two years old. Three years older than Harlan now. It seemed a long time away and yet at the same time, barely enough. He would need to plan every detail to a science.

There could be no mistakes.

He didn't want to end up like Uncle Harlan.

Gerald looked at the ledger one more time before he closed it.

Also by J.P. Choquette

Monsters in the Green Mountains series:
Silence in the Woods
Shadow in the Woods
Under the Mountain
The Pact
Stillwater Lake

Tayt Waters Mystery series:
See No Evil
Hear No Evil

Standalone thrillers:
Let the Dead Rest
Dark Circle
Epidemic

Acknowledgments

Writing might be a solitary task, but it takes a proverbial village to get a book out into the world.

My grateful thanks to my readers and for all the kind sentiments you've shared after reading my other books.

Deep thanks as always to my editor, Helen, for her great work and comments that made me laugh out loud during an otherwise unpleasant process. I value your input and take responsibility for any leftover typos.

Thank you especially to Erin Chagnon, my beta reading champion. You always have such great insights and feedback to offer—I value your sharp eye and wit. Anna Wheeler, Ann Kalinowski, and Kayla James, my gratitude for each of you for taking the time to share your ideas, questions, and thoughts on the manuscript. You all made this book better.

As always, my deepest thanks and appreciation to Serge and Pascal. Our "research trips" in the woods, your creative ideas to plot-related problems, and your support of me mean so much.

Finally, much thankfulness to God for blessing me with any writing talent I have.

~Dios Amore~

About the Author

Thriller author, J.P. Choquette, writes suspense novels with themes of nature, art, and folklore. When she's not working, you'll find her sipping a hot beverage, reading, or in the woods with her family.

Join her Reader's Club and get peeks into her writing life, upcoming releases, and other treats for book lovers.

You can connect with me on:

- https://www.jpchoquette.me
- https://www.instagram.com/jpchoquette_author/?hl=en

Subscribe to my newsletter:

- https://landing.mailerlite.com/webforms/landing/v2g2d5

Printed in the USA
CPSIA information can be obtained
at www.ICGtesting.com
LVHW091510010924
789859LV00008B/297